Scorched Earth

Lying on his belly on the soft cool earth with his MG to one side of him and a prepped Armbrust to the other, Billy McKay cocked his head and listened. The wind shifted slightly, and he heard it clearly: the unmistakable clattering rumble of armor on the roll. *It's never gonna work,* McKay thought. Four hard-core heroes and a pack of amateurs, no matter how inspired, wasn't enough to beat a baker's dozen of AFVs and a short company of troops.

The V-150 in the lead rose a meter in the air on a cushion of white brilliance. For a moment it just hovered there in midair as if it had decided to become a hovercraft. Then it fell over on its right side, skidding five meters in a scream of sparks. And blew up.

The whole thing happened in an awful dead stillness. Then the sound of the mine blast hit McKay full in the face, and he shouted, *"Do it to it!"*

He pressed the trigger. The Armbrust spat its plastic counterweight out one end and a fat shaped-charge rocket out the other. A few meters from the launcher the main propellant kicked in and the rocket went buzzing off toward the rear of the column.

Rockets streaked for the column like a meteor shower rotated ninety degrees. A direct hit sent the commander of the thi̶r̶d̶ ̶u̶n̶i̶t̶?̶ ̶u̶p̶w̶a̶r̶d̶ on a spurt of flame like a cork̶ ̶f̶r̶o̶m̶ ̶a̶ ̶c̶h̶a̶m̶- pagne bottle.

THE GUARDIANS

DESOLATION ROAD

RICHARD AUSTIN

A JOVE BOOK

THE GUARDIANS: DESOLATION ROAD

A Jove Book / published by arrangement with
the author

PRINTING HISTORY
Jove edition / June 1987

ISBN: 0-515-09004-2

Jove Books are published by The Berkley Publishing Group,
200 Madison Avenue, New York, NY 10016.
The words "A JOVE BOOK" and the "J" with sunburst
are trademarks belonging to Jove Publications, Inc.

PRINTED IN THE UNITED STATES OF AMERICA

CHAPTER
ONE ──────────────────

"The accused, Theron Leodore McDonald, is hereby found guilty of possession of an unauthorized automatic weapon," the fat man in horn-rimmed glasses and a slightly grimy white robe intoned, pretending to read from a scroll held myopically close to his nose. The flicker of the torches ringing the clearing reflected in the lenses of his glasses; bullfrogs boomed the bass line to a buzzing cicada chorus. "Has the accused any last words before sentence is executed?"

"I demand a retrial," said the black young man who stood on the lowered tailgate of a Chevy pickup, which was hiked way the hell up on its suspension and had been equipped with tires the size of a 737's. Split, puffed lips mangled the words, and eyes swollen almost shut from a savage beating blunted the effect of the defiant glare he swung around the twenty or thirty heavily armed white men gathered in a semicircle facing the tupelo gum tree under which the pickup was parked. His right arm was in a sling. The left was tied behind his back. A noose of slick nylon rope was draped around his skinny neck.

A burly man with a ginger beard and mustache bronzed by flamelight stood beside the tailgate of the truck, turning over an M-249 Squad Automatic Weapon in his blocky hands. "Theron, you always been a good boy. What got into you, made you think you could get away with carrying around a machine gun like this? We got gun control in these parts."

"There was this little matter of a war goin' on," Theron said, swaying a little in the grasp of the two burly, hooded men who held his arms. "We'd been invaded, like."

"Let's hurry up and hang him, Luther. These damn robes is hot and the mosquitoes is eatin' my face all to shit," somebody in the crowd said. A face like a red balloon poked expectantly out the driver's window of the truck as the executioner craned for the word to let in the clutch. But the big man shook his head.

"No, we Regulators're dedicated to restorin' law and order and the American way of life. We got to do things right and proper."

They weren't exactly the Ku Klux Klan, which had never been too popular in southern Louisiana anyway, though they'd stolen heavily from Klan rituals and regalia. But they were too much into KKK mumbo-jumbo to be out-and-out vigilantes. They were roughnecks, rednecks, cashiered cops, and marginal employables, who had wandered down into the bayou country after the bombs got New Orleans and the plague decimated Baton Rouge and set themselves up as lords and masters over the folk struggling to wring a living out of the green and black and soggy land. Their hooded robes and midnight murders made them seem a lot fancier than they really were. What they mostly were was goons.

And they had come down hard when the young black came home a hero, sporting a wound and an automatic weapon acquired during the recent fight with the Federated States of Europe force that had landed in Terrebonne Bay to seize control of the top-secret Project Starshine lab and its miracle fusion-power generator. The Regulators, however, knew nothing of FSE invasions. Whenever they tried sticking their noses too far south the Cajuns whipped their asses, so mostly they stayed well north of Thibodaux and east of the swamps of the Atchafalaya Basin, and consequently had missed the fun, though they'd gotten their share of the hurricane which finally put paid to the Effsee endeavor.

What the Regulators did know from was that it was not in line with their plans to have uppity niggers wandering around loose with heavy-duty armament. So they had paid a little visit to the McDonald house. The hero's welcome-home celebration had been well under way when the masked men, armed with shotguns and assault rifles, had busted in. Their earlier object lessons had taken effect, it seemed—it wasn't even necessary to shoot any coons as they dragged Theron and his booty off into the night.

Now Luther lowered the M-249's bipod and set it carefully on the ground at his feet. "It don't have to be this way, Theron," he said, almost gently. "All you got to do is tell us who else might have acquired some *il*legal weapons and you go free."

"And the Guardians, Luther, don't forget the Guardians," an adenoidal young voice said from behind.

"Shut up, Willie Earl. Yeah, and if you have any information pertainin' to the whereabouts of the so-called

Guardians, who are wanted for trespass and carryin' of unauthorized weaponry, there might be something extra in it for you.''

"Fuck your mama, Luther. She the only one who'd have you anyway," said Theron.

Luther's pitted face went white behind his beard. "All right, nigger, if that's the way you want it—" He raised his arm.

"Hold on a minute, here, everybody," a voice said from behind. "Let's not do anything you're all gonna regret."

Hoods turned. A man had emerged from the darkness among trees. A large man, with the thick chest and wide shoulders of a lineman. Gold highlights glinted in hair cropped close to his head, which was scarcely—if any —wider than his neck. He wore coveralls dabbed with green and brown and tan camouflage patterns. His brow and chin were massive, his nose broken, his eyes squinted. His lips were wrapped around a stub cigar and a great big grin.

But the most commanding feature of his appearance wasn't his size, or his battered face. It was the big black machine gun he held in both hands, with a half-moon-shaped magazine hung on the side of a humpbacked receiver, rifle stock tucked under one arm, fore and rear pistols grips held in huge scarred hands. The Regulators gathered in the clearing for a little rough post-holocaust justice believed as fervently in Sylvester Stallone as they did in the thunder-and-napalm gospel broadcast by the Reverend Nathan Bedford Forrest Smith from his stronghold in Oklahoma City, so the brighter among them even recognized the weapon from its cameo appearance as a captured Soviet machine gun in *Rambo*. Actually, it was a Maremont Lightweight Machine Gun, military designation M-60E3, and as American as pizza and chop suey. And it was held in very unauthorized hands.

"Just who the hell do you think you are?" the moon-faced man in glasses demanded.

"I think I'm Billy McKay of the Guardians," the apparition said around his cigar. "And I think I got the drop on a lot of detached assholes."

"Hey, Luther," the skinny kid with the M-16 slung over his back said excitedly. "Hey, I bet he's one of them dudes like we ran into a couple weeks back—"

McKay turned to regard the ginger-bearded man, who stood a good two inches taller than his six-three. "Yeah. And you must be the two Sam Sloan put the fear of God into with his little grenade trick." A red flush crept up out of the robe and crawled all over Luther's face. "I figured you Regulators couldn't amount to much, to let a Navy boy run your asses like that. I see I was right."

He gestured with the M-60. "I'm gettin' tired of small talk. Cut him down."

Luther stood there with his jaw working like a kitten under a blanket. He was no coward, just a man with a fine appreciation of the odds. The shorter, round-faced man presiding over the ceremony was of different stuff. Since the One-Day War he'd found a whole new life browbeating the unarmed and the helpless, people too pounded down by disaster to make any kind of effective stand against Regulator inroads. It had given him kind of a skewed perspective as to just how things ought to go.

"What are you men thinking of?" he demanded, starting around with his fire blanked lenses. "There's twenty, thirty of us here, and just one of him."

"He got him a machine gun," Luther pointed out.

"We got guns." Which was true, but most of them were slung, and those who happened to have long arms in the hand had developed a marked tendency to stare at the ground or off into the trees and hold the pieces as if they weren't sure what they were or how they happened to have hold of them.

Seeing his companions were not exactly closing ranks behind him, the round-faced man smiled. "Well, we still got something you want," he said, "and I aim to make sure you don't get it. Rollie, fire her up—*make that nigger dance!*" And he whipped a Smith & Wesson .38 out from under his robes and shot Billy McKay in the short ribs.

A lot of things happened at once.

The jacked-up pickup roared and bucked like a bronc busting out of the gate and shot right out from under Theron McDonald. He dropped—clear to the ground, where the nylon rope coiled around him, cleanly severed by a gunshot no one had heard.

Billy McKay staggered from the bullet's impact. It was a soft lead hollowpoint, which made even a piss-poor pistol like a .38 stone death to frightened swampers with just their shirts between them and it, but it never even had a chance of punching through the Kevlar vest McKay wore under his coveralls. In fact it splashed so comprehensively that its force was spread out over McKay's side, sparing him much of the effect of even a well-stopped round.

But he still felt as if he had been smacked with a hammer. "Sonofabitch," McKay grunted, and fired.

Huge and muscular as he was, he was almost able to hold the heavy barrel down against the recoil. Almost. The 7.62 millimeter slugs scattered red holes from the crotch of the moonfaced man's robe to his shoulder. They passed through his body so quickly they barely rocked him. When McKay's finger came off the trigger Moonface collapsed like an empty suit slipping from a hanger in the sudden sledgehammer silence.

Burly Luther had dived and was rolling away, the M-249 in his hands. About half the assembled Regulators had decided discretion was the better part of vigilantedom and were rabbiting into the dark. The other half realized that, well armed though he was, the interloper was just one man—as well as thinking that the revolver bullet had gone home, and the bullet spray that had answered it was the reflex response of a gut-shot man. They smelled blood, and numbers made them brave.

McKay spun right round, firing from the hip. His burst whirled adenoidal Willie Earl out from behind his M-16 like a weathercock. A man just behind him fired his Remington riot gun, missed, and McKay cut him down. But a burst of full-auto fire cracked past him from behind, and Luther was getting his big body settled down behind the Squad Automatic Weapon with disconcerting familiarity. McKay's shit, in a word, was weak.

From out in the words came a big hollow *pop* like an M-80 going off in a trashcan. Something thumped on the soft ground under the tupelo gum and began to hiss off a cloud of white smoke right in Luther's bearded face.

"Gas!" a Regulator shouted, as the white smoke plunged jagged fingers down his throat. Panicked vigilantes staggered weeping and choking into the trees.

The woods bloomed with yellow muzzle flashes. Robed figures fell screaming and kicking chunks out of the mushy earth. The executioner ran his pickup smack into a tree, whose bole cracked loudly but held. He boiled out of the driver's door, cutting loose onehanded with a short MAC-10 submachine gun. Squinting against the tear gas that seemed to be clawing at his eyes, McKay pivoted, fired from the hip, and knocked the executioner sprawling.

Every Regulator who could headed for tall timber. From off in the black woods came shots, shouts, screams and curses, the firefly winks of muzzle blasts, and now and again the big flash and doorslam sound of a grenade going off. The fleeing Regulators were clearly running afoul of some kind of force encircling the clearing.

"Just don't seem to be their day," Theron McDonald observed. He had worked himself up to a sitting position. The tear gas had passed him by.

McKay rubbed his eyes. "Almost wasn't your day, kid."

"Hey, man, all's well that ends well."

The CS gas didn't last long in the humid air. McKay's eyes streamed, but his vision was clear as men in jungle cammies and U.S. Army Kevlar helmets shaped like coal scoops poured into the clearing. A black man with a sergeant's chevrons and a darker spot on the upper arm of his cammie blouse, as if a circular patch had recently been peeled away, walked up to McKay and saluted.

"And just where the goddam hell were you?" McKay bellowed. His face had turned an interesting shade of magenta. *"I coulda got my ass shot off waiting for you pukes."*

"Took longer than expected to get into position," Staff Sergeant Gates, late of the FSE, said, unmoved. "This was a pretty improvised sort of thing."

Theron McDonald was staring up at his rescuers with his forehead wrinkled in surprise and suspicion. "Hey, what's goin' on? You're Effees, ain't you? Same dudes shot me in the arm in the first place. You switch sides an' shit?"

Several soldiers securing the wounded Regulators growled at that.

"We're on the same side we always were," the sergeant said evenly. "America's. Just turned out we were a mite confused as to just where her best interests lay."

Out in the woods the firefight sounds were dying back. "Some of them are getting away, Billy," the soft voice of Tom Rogers drawled over the tiny speaker taped to the mastoid bone behind McKay's ear. "Want us to chase 'em?"

"What do *you* say?" McKay said—not speaking aloud, but subvocalizing for the benefit of the microphone taped to his larynx.

A few years ago, former sergeant and drill instructor McKay would have been shocked at the very idea of asking a subordinate what orders he ought to give him. But the Guardians weren't just your normal grunts. They were supersoldiers, four men picked from among the millions in America's armed forces and subjected to the most exacting training in military history. They worked as a team, a smoothly functioning, integrated unit.

"Let 'em go. We don't need our boys stumbling around in the swamps, and the Regulators won't stop running this side of Vicksburg." A veteran of the U.S. Army Special Forces—the Green Berets—Guardian Rogers had years of experience serving as cadre for indigenous resistance forces in half a dozen Third World trouble spots.

"Do that," McKay said.

A man in camouflaged coveralls identical to McKay's, if less capacious, ambled into the torchlight. He was carrying a bull-barreled Remington 700 bolt-action rifle with an outsized telescopic sight. He wore a baseball cap with the name and logo of the rock group Heart on it, and yellow Zeiss shooting glasses. He was tall, if not as tall as McKay, rangy, and handsome in a boyish way. The hair strapped at an angle across his forehead by the cap's sweatband was blond and straight.

"Hi, Theron," he said to the captive.

"Hey, Case, what's happenin', man?"

Grounding the rifle's metal buttplate Casey Wilson hunkered down beside McDonald and examined the severed rope end with keen interest. "Got it in one shot," he said with satisfaction in his oh-wow Southern California accent. "I always wanted to do that. Ever since I, like, saw *The Good, the Bad, and the Ugly*." He was the team's driver and sniper. Before becoming a Guardian he'd only been the best fighter jock in the world.

"You shot the rope in two?" Theron said in disbelief.

"Yeah, man."

"Jesus *Christ*. What if you'd missed the damn rope?"

A self-deprecating shrug. "Wasn't all that hard a shot, man."

Young McDonald's face had turned the shade of burnt-down charcoal. Casey was sawing at the rope cutting off circulation to his hands with a leaf-bladed Gerber Mark II. When the bonds fell away Theron hopped up and tore the inexpertly tied noose free and threw it into the woods.

"Never cared for no necktie, anyway," he said. "Look, man, it ain't that I ain't grateful. But how'd you happen along at just the right moment? Seems to be, like, stretching coincidence, if you know what I mean."

Former expeditionary force troopies, white ones grinning and black ones grinning wider, were herding Regulators—whose own faces were a few shades lighter than the sheets they wore—into the clearing.

"Your pals were a little overconfident," McKay said, holding his Maremont with one hand while massaging his ribs with the other. "They forgot to look for the CB radio your mama had in the back room. They weren't out of sight before she was on the horn calling for help, just like we told folks to do."

"How'd you find me?"

Gates laughed. "Shit, everybody around here knows where the Regulators hold their midnight parties. Besides, we caught a latecomer on the road. He told us just where to find you, after Tom Rogers had a little talk with him." A master of field interrogation techniques, Rogers disapproved of the use of torture, mainly because it lacked finesse. On the other hand, he wasn't averse to describing to the captive a few of the things he *could* do, if he had a mind to. Things he'd heard from people like Pathans who'd fought the Soviets in the Khyber Pass. The captive had stood about three minutes of it and spilled his guts.

"What we gonna do with these dudes, Sarge?" asked a black soldier with a full-sized M-60 riding on a sling.

Gates looked at McKay. "They're your prisoners. I'd like to suggest you let the locals work something out, though. Discourage atrocities, but shit, don't sweat it too much."

Tom Rogers walked in with the rest of the prisoners. He carried an M-79 grenade launcher shaped something like a fat sawed-off shotgun. Behind him walked a short Chicano holding on to a rope. The other end of the rope was knotted around Luther's muscular neck. The Regulator boss's face looked as if it had been remodeled some with a rifle butt since McKay had seen him last.

"He gave us some shit when we caught him," the squaddie said in reply to McKay's questioning look. "I figured he was tryin' to escape, but you said to take as many prisoners as we could, so—'' He shrugged.

Hands on hips, Theron strutted up to the burly bearded man. "You always been a sonofabitch, Luther, but maybe we can put you to use. Diggin' latrines be about your speed. Maybe if you behave yourself, we'll give you a shovel."

"You're gonna pay for this, nigger," Luther gritted, and spat out a flake of tooth.

"No, motherfucker. I already paid. Now I gon' *collect*."

"Guardians, this is Starshine," the voice of Sam Sloan, the fourth member of the team, said in McKay's ear. The words were blurred with distance. "Guardians, this is Starshine, do you read?"

McKay gestured for Gates's radioman; the backpack unit was needed to boost the sending power of their pocket-calculator–sized communicators to reach clear to Wolf Bayou in the depths of the Atchafalaya. "Starshine, this is McKay. We read you five-by, over."

"Guardians, return to Starshine soonest. I say again, return at once."

"What's up, Sam?" asked Casey, who didn't have much use for standard radio procedure unless he was strapped at the cockpit of an F-16.

"Washington was just on the horn. The Federated States of Europe have been invaded, and everything's hit the fan!"

CHAPTER
TWO ⎯⎯⎯⎯⎯⎯⎯⎯⎯⎯⎯

"Iskander Bey," said Dr. Marguerite Connoly.

"Gesundheit," Billy McKay said, easing his bulk back in the comfortless chair in the dead-air blandness of the briefing chamber beneath the White House. The only sounds that managed to penetrate the subterranean womb were the slightly arrhythmic thumping of the inadequate air conditioning and, faintly, the sounds of the mostly Asian work crews from Soong's camp on the Tidal Basin restoring the structure to a semblance of its former glory. The dim busy sounds reassured him; being stuck down here in apparently total isolation made him feel like he was in one of those movies where all of humanity has been wiped out, except for a handful of survivors holed up in a bunker.

Not that being holed up in a doomsday bunker with his three fellow teammates would be so bad. Even being stuck with Tide Camp boss soldier Steve Tyler (currently acting as military advisor to President Jeffrey

MacGregor) wasn't too terrible a fate, even though
Tyler now had his hair all roached up and dyed pine-
apple yellow at the bottom and Ronald Reagan orange
on top, and wore Bermuda shorts and these batwing
shades whose lenses glistened green like a fly's ab-
domen, as though he were nostalgically trying to recre-
ate the punk fashions of his youth, but that was just the
way the Tide Camp boys were, even a combat vet like
Tyler. And that little assistant of Connoly's, standing
up next to the doctor and Tyler at the head of the phony
walnut-paneled table looking desperately prim in a subdued mauve skirt suit and gray stockings—*wonder how
she walks through the rubble in them heels?*—being
cooped up with her wouldn't be terrible *at all,* even if
she needed some makeup and didn't have much in the
way of boobs.

No. The prospect that sent cold sweat seeping down
McKay's spine was the vision of being locked up in the
last bunker in the world with Maggie Connoly, formerly
professor of economics at Harvard, now chief advisor
to the President of the United States. Now *that* was a
nightmare.

Right now she tipped her snub nose down and gave
him a look over the round tops of her glasses, the sort of
look a high school teacher gives the class slug when he
belches in the middle of an explanation of quadratic
equations. " 'Iskander Bey' is the name taken by the in-
dividual who is at this moment leading an invasion of
Europe by Muslin fundamentalist fanatics," she said
coldly. "Ms. Scowcroft will explain the historical refer-
ents, for those who are completely ignorant on the subject."

The young woman moistened her lips. " 'Iskander
Bey' means 'Lord Alexander.' It's the Arabic name for
Alexander the Great. It's considered an auspicious name

for a conqueror, for obvious reasons, and through history has frequently been assumed by men with military ambitions in various parts of the Arab-speaking world. The current holder of the name is a Turkish soldier who served at one time with NATO, General Hafiz Tulul. He claims to have experienced an epiphany in which the Prophet endowed him with the destiny to overthrow the Western infidels.''

''But the Turks are our allies,'' Sam Sloan exclaimed. He was sitting up straight and taking notes like a good little boy.

Tyler laughed, pushed his shades down his skinny nose. ''If you'd served on the ground in the Med, rather than safe and snug on that iron bathtub of yours, you'd know just how little that matters. I would need a calculator to figure out all the times I came near being scragged by our ostensible friends, from the Brits, French, and Swedes through the Israelis and the Saudis. Just about as often as I wound up working with our enemies, and not just Syrians and Iranians but Soviets too, once or twice. I see you looking skeptical, sailor boy. Am I bullshitting, McKay?''

''No bullshit.''

Blond-haired Melissa Scowcroft was looking peeved by the interruption but as if she didn't quite dare to speak up. Connoly did. ''Gentlemen,'' she said briskly, ''if I may be forgiven the loose use of the term, might we possibly return to the subject at hand, and leave off swaggering until you can adjourn with a sigh of relief to the locker room and snap each other's jocks to your heart's content?''

Sloan's handsome rectangular face flushed. Tyler laughed, cocked his finger on his thumb, and snapped his glasses back in place. ''You got the stage, Melissa, honey.''

She nipped quickly at her underlip, began tentatively, "In recent years an upsurge of the Shia sect of Islam in Turkey and the USSR has allied itself with Pan-Turanianism, a movement to unite all the Turkic peoples of Asia, which was suppressed by the Soviets in the twenties. The Turks are traditionally regarded with disfavor by their Arabic and Iranian coreligionists, but the success of the Pan-Turanians in destabilizing the Soviet Union in the years before the Third World War earned the movement substantial cachet among Muslims everywhere. That, combined with an upsurge of religious fervor following the war, has produced conditions favorable to a jihad against the infidels, which is to say the West and the remnants of the USSR, the Great Satans of the Islamic fundamentalists."

"I thought the United States was the Great Satan," Sam said.

"You think the Shiites can tell us and the Russians apart, bunky?" Tyler hooted. "They'd say anything to anybody to get guns and aid—lying in the cause of the faith's part of their beliefs, look it up—but they hate the Commies just as much as they do us."

Tyler swung his Ho Chi Minh–slippered feet up onto the tabletop and whipped a pointer up to tap on the map of Europe hung on the wall behind him. "Is it okay if I talk now, Mother?"

Connoly got a pinched look on her round face, but said nothing.

"Right. How this effects us is like this. What we got is, this General Tulul—Iskander Bey—is pushing up from Turkey into the Balkans—here." He stabbed with a pointer without looking back. "Have I got it?"

"Looks like France to me, man," said Casey, flaked bonelessly out in a chair at the foot of the table.

Tyler glanced back, started to lose his balance, caught

himself, and snapped the pointer to the appropriate spot. "I knew that. So anyway, Iskander Baby's driving into Greece and Bulgaria, which are pretty mountainous and in general a pain in the ass. But we got reports, straight from the horse's mouth—" He meant the satellite links that carried Federated States in Europe, which the Guardians' hacker friends in the Freehold and occupied California had tapped into, thanks to the passwords and recognition codes the Guardians had liberated with their current armored car, Mobile One. "—that there've been landings on the Rumanian coast, at the mouths of the Danube, and up near Odessa in the Ukraine."

McKay winched up a pale eyebrow. "Amphibious assaults? These religious nuts got some pretty boss equipment."

"Not really. They're coming in on tramp steamers, fellucas, rowboats—unimaginable shit, from the reports we're getting. Just hordes and hordes of fanatics swarming ashore with everything from scimitars to RPG-16s. Of course, they do have some armor with the LSTs to bring it in with, courtesy of NATO.

"Well, the Balkans and the Ukraine are both supposedly part of the FSE, but that wouldn't worry our buddy Maximov much. If the *mujahideen* want to break into Western Europe through the mountains, there's nothing his turncoat NATO and Warsaw Pact troopies can't handle.

"But here's the kicker: that attack on the Black Sea's only part of it. Landings have been reported from Spain clear to Yugoslavia, and the local Effsee commanders are crying their heads off for help from Málaga to Trieste. Nobody knows whether these are just raids, diversions, or major thrusts; on-the-spot reports give huge numbers for the invaders, but we all know how that works. What's clear is that this new jihad poses a big threat to the existence of Chairman Maximov's empire.''

McKay opened his mouth for a comment along the lines of what-the-fuck's-this-got-to-do-with-*us?* Connoly leaped on the lull and wrestled it to the carpet.

"What this jihad offers,'' she said hurriedly, "is an unparalleled opportunity for us.''

Silence spread out from her like oil poured onto a pond.

"Okay, I'll bite,'' McKay said, taking a cigar from the pocket of his silver-gray fatigue coveralls and biting off the tip. "What kind of opportunity?''

"Lieutenant McKay, I'll thank you not to light that in here,'' Connoly said pointedly.

"You won't get the chance,'' McKay said. He flicked a lighter and puffed the cigar into noxious life.

"Yes, what kind of opportunity does this turn of events offer us?'' Sam asked too loudly, as the muscles of Connoly's face worked angrily. She got herself under control with effort.

"The opportunity to liberate the state of California and drive the last of the Federated States of Europe invaders from American soil.''

McKay choked and jackknifed forward, spitting his cigar onto the pale carpet. Casey pounded him enthusiastically on the back until McKay batted his hand away. "Enough! Don't karate chop me, goddamn it, you're gonna bust my spine.''

"I'm sorry, Billy, I was only trying to help,'' Casey said, looking crestfallen behind his inevitable yellow Zeiss glasses.

"Yeah, yeah.'' McKay bent down, recovered the cigar, and stuck it back in his face. "Somebody musta slipped me a hash cigar, 'cause I thought I just heard you say something about liberating California from the fucking Effsees."

Melissa Scowcroft went a shade paler, whether at the language or the tone directed at her boss McKay couldn't tell and didn't care.

Connoly stuck her fists on her hips. "What's the matter, Lieutenant McKay? I thought you were quite the super soldier, always arrogant, always confident. Does the prospect frighten you?"

McKay's bull neck swelled until it seemed wider than his close-cropped head, and a vein pulsed on his forehead. He settled himself back at an angle in the chair, crossed a boot over his knee, and chewed on his cigar.

"Lemme put it to you this way, Doc," he rasped. "The Effsees have ten thousand men worth of expeditionary force on the ground in California. Now, just to show how arrogant I really am, I'll say each of us Guardians is worth a hundred Effsees, even Sam Sloan, and him a college boy and all. Shit, I'll make it a *thousand* of the motherfuckers. Yes, ma'am, each one of us Guardians is worth one thousand of these Effsee pukes."

He blew out a stream of smoke. "And that only leaves six thousand of 'em unaccounted for. Am I getting through to you, Maggie?"

"Billy's right," said Tom Rogers flatly. "We can do a lot. But only a fool'd think we could make much impression on ten thousand Effsees."

"Meaning me, Lieutenant Rogers?" Connoly asked, eyeing him stonily.

Rogers just looked back with his shark-gray eyes and worked his jaw around.

To the Guardians' surprise Connoly laughed. "I certainly got your attention, didn't I? There's more to the scenario than you've heard . . . which you can hear now, if you're sure you're finished jumping to conclusions.''

"That's most of the exercise I've gotten the last three weeks, jumping to conclusions," Sloan drawled.

Connoly turned him a look that was not amused.

Sloan grimaced. Much as he respected Dr. Connoly's credentials she made him feel uncomfortable, like an unruly schoolboy.

"Ah, right." Tyler swiveled his makeshift sandals off the table and stood, going up on his toes briefly as if stretching out his hamstrings. "Now, I admit the situation looks a little shaggy from the point of view you've been taking. But remember you're not being asked to operate in a vacuum."

"This is true," McKay said. "Ten thousand Effsees is in fact your basic crowded environment, it seems to me."

"I gather you gentlemen simply wish to write off California, then?" Connoly asked with venomous sweetness.

Sloan's lips became a bloodless line. The image of Susan Spinelli flashed into his mind—the blond, lithe, assistant director of the New Eden agricultural laboratory and commune, which was currently occupied by the FSE expeditionary force. The other Guardians traded angry looks. Connoly was prodding them in a sore spot, the fact that they'd so far done nothing about the occupation of California.

"Listen, lady," McKay said. "We want the fuckin' Effsees out of America as much as anybody. We just know the four of us can't drive them out by ourselves.

"But it ain't like we're not gonna do what we can to make their lives miserable. It's just that we been a bit busy these last few months. Otherwise we'd be out there right now, kickin' asses and takin' names. Makin' what trouble we could. We got some friends the Effsees are squatting on.''

Connoly nodded smugly. She had them on the defensive now. "So I gather you are willing to take steps against the FSE forces in California."

"Shit, yeah," McKay said. "We're ready to go and fuck with their infrastructure, bushwhack their tax collectors, blow up their motor pool, bol bean their ammo stocks, drop big rocks on their convoys, the whole nine yards."

" 'Bol bean'?" Melissa Scowcroft asked. She had great eyes, very green and somewhat slanted over prominent cheekbones. *Too bad she keeps lookin' at me like I smell bad,* McKay thought.

"He means replacing their ammunition with cartridges loaded with high explosives," Tom Rogers explained. "When they fire their pieces, it blows their faces off, ma'am."

Scowcroft blanched. Connoly never turned a hair. McKay had to admit that while she looked like some kind of Sierra Club schoolteacher, with her round face and fit, stocky body, the jeans and L. L. Bean shirts she liked to wear, her round snub-nosed face and curly graying hair and wire-rimmed glasses, she was tough as Kevlar.

"Anyway," McKay went on, "we can do all that, but it adds up to jack. We can pry the Effsees' fingers off pieces of real estate here and there, but when it comes to this talk about 'liberating California,' we are entering the Twilight Zone."

Tyler stuck his hands in the pockets of his improbably baggy and garish shorts. "I think you're forgetting a basic point here, Lieutenant."

"Yeah? Like what?"

"Like the invasion of Europe by Islamic looney-tunes."

CHAPTER
THREE ━━━━━━━━━━━━━

"Keep talkin', McKay urged.

"You don't think when this Iskander sinks his teeth into our buddy Maximov's butt that he ain't gonna think of a better use for ten thousand troopies than sitting in the sun at Malibu?"

"Are you saying Chairman Maximov is withdrawing the expeditionary force?" Sloan asked.

"No. What I am saying is that he may, and you have the chance to encourage him to do just that. Go out to California, raise maximum hell, do all the things you were talking about. I understand you're a real wizard at raising guerrillas, Tom—"

The square-set ex–Green Beret sat looking at him with level eyes, not responding. "Yeah. He is," McKay said.

"So okay. Go for it. Our sources in California indicate that Maitland isn't waging the battle for hearts and minds with too much success—"

"Not without Ivan Vesensky to tell him how," Sloan said.

"—so you can probably whip up enough insurrections to run them out of their shorts. You can make their lives very, very unhappy, gentlemen."

He held up his hands to ward off objections. "I'm not saying any of this is going to amount to kicking their asses out of California. But if you put it together with the crisis in Europe, you just might help them decide to vacate the premises voluntarily."

The Guardians could almost see a harsh glint of eagerness through Tyler's weird bluebottle shades. Bizarre as they were, as much trouble as they'd given the Guardians when they first brought Jeff MacGregor back to the D.C. rubble, the men of Tide Camp were true believers, who had kept the flame alight through the long year since the war—maintaining the White House against looters and squatters, a shrine almost, undefiled for the President's return. The presence of the Effsees was almost as personal an affront to them as to the Guardians.

But not quite. Each man of the Guardians had a personal score to settle with the Federated States of Europe, and each was a long one. But they were swapping uncertain glances. McKay, Sloan, even stolid Rogers and laid-back California kid Casey Wilson felt the prospect of actually coming to grips with the expeditionary force in a finish fight hit their veins like mainlined speed. But still, the Guardians didn't just go racing into things.

"If possible," Marguerite Connoly said into silence, "it would be advisable to keep participation by armed civilians to a minimum. Perhaps you could encourage acts of passive resistance on the part of the populace. I deplore the notion of violent resistance."

McKay tipped his head to one side and gave Tyler the fish eye. "Is this one for real, Tyler?"

"Why don't you, like, tell the doctor how well passive resistance has been working in the Federated States of Europe?" Casey suggested blandly to Tyler.

Tyler threw back his head and his skinny Adam's apple jerked to a caw of laughter. "Works great. Quickest form of suicide known to man. You know how they used to use high-pressure firehoses for crowd control, Doc? Well, before the rebellion broke out in Antwerp last year they didn't fuck around with that stuff. They used flamethrowers."

Connoly's mouth rumpled and she prodded at the rim of her glasses with a forefinger. "Surely you don't credit such rumors—"

"Rumors my skinny white ass. I helped interrogate some of the Effsees we caught when they tried to crash us in August. These pukes play for keeps. All an unarmed populace is gonna give 'em is target practice."

"Very well," Connoly said, without enthusiasm. "You gentlemen may take whatever steps you find . . . expedient . . . in seeing to the removal of Federated States of Europe forces from American soil." She consulted the LCD screen of a notebook computer sitting on the table before her. "According to reports, your vehicle is fully outfitted and ready to go. You'll leave immediately—"

"Not so fast," Sam Sloan said.

"Just who the hell are you to go giving us orders, Doctor?" McKay growled.

She reared back like a plump irritable cobra. "I'm a duly appointed representative of the President of the United States."

"Bullshit," McKay said.

Scowcroft gasped. Connoly stared at him, nostrils

slightly flared, as if unable to believe he'd had the temerity to interrupt her. Beneath anger flat and hard and cold as the top of an unlit iron stove he wondered if she was maybe half-bright; surely she knew what he was like by now.

She gathered her composure back around her. "Are you questioning orders from the President, Lieutenant McKay?"

"He's questioning instructions from a civilian whose position in the chain of command is decidedly less than obvious to the naked eye," said Sam Sloan. Gone was the amiable aw-shucks Jim Garner Missouri shitkicker; in his place sat the Icy Commander, Annapolis-trained autocrat with eyes unflinching as death.

"We're not part of the TO&E of the regular armed forces, ma'am," Tom Rogers said, respectfully but firmly. "And we don't take orders from civilians."

"We're an independent outfit," Casey added. "We only answer to the President."

Connoly stared at them with a face like mud baked hard by the sun. "This is insubordination of the rankest kind—"

"This is a top-secret operation, Doctor," Casey said, and his grin was for once not at all pleasant or laid-back. "Like, how about showing us your security clearance?" He was not usually the type to put much stock in that sort of thing, but he was having fun right now.

Connoly flushed. "I assure you, I enjoy the President's utmost confidence—"

"I'm sure you do, Doctor," Sloan said. "So do we. And he's never mentioned putting us in your charge."

Clearly outflanked, and no fool, the economist looked around for reinforcements. Her assistant was standing by gazing at the Guardians with fixed eyes, breath coming in short gasps, clearly overstressed by the high-tension emotion that charged the briefing chamber. And Tyler merely showed her an infuriating impudent grin when she turned to him.

"From where I sit, you look like a civilian trying to boss soldiers. There's only one who gets to do that. Or perhaps you figure some of the President's authority has rubbed off on you?"

Dr. Connoly turned red, then white, and then her eyes were turned toward the murky pastel carpet and her fingers fumbled with the rims of her round glasses. "I—I'm going to have to consult with the President on this matter," she said. "It's possible I've misinterpreted his directives."

She gathered up her papers into a leather portfolio and marched out of the room. Her assistant gave the Guardians a final hard, if unfocused, stare, and then followed.

"Whoo. That's one tough bitch," Tyler remarked. He looked back at the Guardians. "So you're not going to California?"

"Like fuck we're not," said Billy McKay.

It was all, as Dr. Connoly explained, with what were —for her—profuse apologies, an unfortunate misunderstanding. Sorely pressed for time by the awesome task of trying to reassert some sort of control over a shattered country from the midst of a rubbled-out capital, President MacGregor had delegated the task of briefing the Guardians to his most trusted aide. There had been no implied delegation of authority over them. Connoly had merely been trying to be helpful and pass on the President's instructions. There had been nothing ominous about any of it.

Right.

"I may be nuts, Tom," McKay said, sitting with his feet propped on the railing of the South Portico, gazing off across the South Lawn and the Ellipse toward the broken-off stump of the Washington Monument, gray stone chromed by the light of a sinking half-moon. Beyond burned the fires of Tide Camp, around the rice paddies where the cherry trees used to bloom. Late-season crickets were cranking it up, and a soft breeze brought a residual tang of ash and fading corruption.

"Big of you to admit it, McKay," remarked Sam Sloan, leaning on the wrought iron railing.

"Fuck off and die, Navy boy. This is serious shit. I have this feeling Doctor Maggie thinks she's sending us off to get our asses shot loose."

"Paranoia," Sloan scoffed. "For God's sake, McKay, Dr. Connoly was one of the most respected people in the country, back before the war."

"So was Dexter White," Casey said. "And look what he did to us."

McKay shot him a look. McKay was worried about him. California was his home, and like Sloan he had a honey back on the West Coast, in his case a tall redhead named Rhoda, a well-built lady who hung out at Balin's Forge on the northern outskirts of L.A. Between that and the chance to get into it with the damned Effsees he should have been soaring like an F-15 blazing off the runway. Instead he seemed to have this dark cloud hovering over him, which was as unlike the Casey Wilson McKay knew as it was possible to be.

"I don't like it." Tom Rogers stood off to the side, out of the light spilling from the brightly lit interior of the White House. Even here, in the midst of nominally safe country, it wasn't his habit to silhouette himself.

Sloan frowned at him.

"That mixup about command," Rogers went on.

"Don't reckon it was accidental."

"For God's sake," said Sloan, exasperated. "Dr. Connoly is a civilian, Tom. She isn't used to our weird military jargon."

Rogers said nothing.

Sloan, earnest as a schoolboy, began to explain to him why it really was nothing more than a misunderstanding; that Dr. Connoly was a comrade in arms and to attribute malice to her was nothing more than sheer craziness . . .

McKay went for a walk. They were moving out for California in the morning, across a continent, which, if no longer occupied by Effsee garrisons, was still very much Indian country. Preoccupied as they'd been with the Effsees, it was easy for them to forget that the whole continent was full of hellraisers and would-be vest-pocket Hitlers who could complicate their mission in unforeseen ways—and who'd still have to be dealt with if and when the whole Effsee thing was resolved.

Then there were the Effsees themselves. Their morale was not great, as they were a polyglot force held together by little more than fear of Maximov's political police, far from home with little hope of reinforcement or resupply even before this invasion thing. But they *were* trained troops, most of them seasoned in action during or since the One-Day War. And there were ten thousand of them.

McKay had lied to Connoly. He wasn't afraid of the Effsees, not even ten thousand of them. He just doubted he and his three comrades, hard-core heroes though they were, could make much of an impression on them.

And no matter what Sam believed, he was a damn sight less than comfortable with Maggie Connoly in his backfield.

A footstep crunching gravel behind him brought him around, crouched, with his hand on the butt of his combat-modified .45. The light of the sinking moon turned the thorny hedges of the Rose Garden into a threatening tangle of shadow, where tricks of light and darkness could hide an assailant until his arm was around your throat and his knife was sawing at your jugular. *Sonofabitch, I knew I shoulda made them level this shit,* he thought wildly, but no, Jeff MacGregor insisted the garden was too fine a relic of former glory to be dispensed with merely to provide clear fields of fire around the White House. McKay made ready for battle or boogieing, whichever seemed called for.

A figure stepped out onto the open pathway. McKay let his hand ease off the black-rubber Pachmayr grips of his .45 as the figure was obviously female, and no random rubble rat of any gender dressed *that* way.

"Lieutenant McKay?" the intruder asked, walking forward. Moonlight was dusted like early snow across the padded shoulders of her jacket and along the curve of skirted hip. An admirable curve, McKay couldn't help noticing.

"Evening, Ms. Scowcroft," McKay grunted around the butt of his cigar. "What brings you out at this time of night? Don't know what you might run into."

Melissa Scowcroft smiled. "Certainly I do. Your friends told me you were out here."

McKay's eyes narrowed. "Me?"

"I wanted to talk to you."

"Didn't think I'd made that good an impression on yuh—uh . . ." The words sort of dribbled off into silence. Melissa Scowcroft had stopped not six feet away, reached for her waist, and let her skirt fall in a pool around her ankles.

"That's, ah, that's a nice garter belt you got there,"

McKay said. "Where'd you find it, anyway?"

She had hung her jacket on a bush and had her frilly blouse most of the way off. The garter belt in question was all she wore, aside from the gray silk stockings and gray shoes and an amused little smile.

"Scavengers scarfed it out of a Frederick's," she replied matter-of-factly, draping the blouse over the jacket and turning to face him. She had an awfully firm body for a high-powered administrative type. Moonlight chased itself through the thicket of her pubic hair.

McKay made a noise in the base of his throat. "What's the occasion?"

"After months being cooped up with a bunch of hay-seeds and hollow-chested scientists, you don't know what a relief it is to find a real man," she said. She stepped up so close he could feel the heat wash off her nude body, and his head throbbed with the hungry moist smell of her.

She reached up, plucked the cigar out of his mouth, and tossed it away. "I don't believe in wasting time."

"Neither do I," McKay growled, and reached for her.

CHAPTER
FOUR ──────────────

Through premature autumn the Guardians drove
west from Washington, D.C., through West Virginia.
They intended to travel through Ohio and Indiana,
switching onto Interstate 80 in Illinois to pass not far
from the crater where Heartland used to be in Iowa, and
from there through Nebraska and Wyoming. Following
80 when it veered southwest past the burnt-out husk of
Rock Springs, their projected route edged between the
ruins of Salt Lake City and Utah Lake, swinging back
onto the highway on the south fringe of the Great Salt
Lake itself. At the Nevada border they would turn
southwest on U.S. Alternate 93, aiming to cut the Sierra
Nevada near Yosemite and enter occupied California.

The route had the advantage of avoiding Missouri
and Oklahoma. The fallout had long since died back to
a few craters pimpling the former missile farms in the
eastern part of Missouri, and farmers had begun to re-
populate the area covered by the lethal roostertails from

Whiteman, scraping topsoil contaminated by residual radiation into big mounds on the edges of their fields and carrying on with life. But to the best of the Guardians' limited knowledge, Dexter White was still mayor of Kansas City, and they enjoyed a certain pride of place on his shitlist.

White was unreasonably irate with them for having shot up his personal citadel and personal bodyguard and then used the mayoral personage itself as a hostage to cover their escape—and all because he had merely set them and Indigo Three up to be surrounded and slaughtered by the Effsees. Though he probably didn't have expeditionary force troopies helping prop him up anymore, he had a healthy private army of his own scraped together from state and local police and National Guard units, who could have made the Guardians' visit to Missouri more interesting than they had in mind.

As for Oklahoma, Sam remarked that avoiding that state was always a fine policy. But the Guardians had a much better reason: former TV boy-wonder evangelist Nathan Bedford Forrest Smith, who ruled the state— much of the Middle West, in fact—from his stronghold in Oklahoma City in the name of the Church of the New Dispensation and its departed First Prophet, Josiah Coffin. White's intentions towards the Guardians were benign in comparison to Reverend Forrie's, as the Guardians had been responsible for the First Prophet's abrupt departure to another and presumably better venue during his abortive crusade against the Freehold in Colorado.

Reverend Forrie was another of those bits of unfinished business the Guardians would have to deal with when the FSE threat was settled, presuming always that it was. He was perhaps the major power in the continental U.S. aside from the Effsees, commanding vastly

greater resources than Jeff MacGregor hunkering in the
ruins of the nation's capital. He had adherents everywhere his radio station, KFSU, reached—which was
everywhere—and he had managed to keep alive the peculiar mésalliance the First Prophet had achieved between the faithful and numerous gangs of road gypsies,
the nomad bandits who'd terrorized the nation's high-
ways even before the big balloon went up. More to the
point, he'd been the first—and loudest—leader of post-
war America to hail the return of Wild Bill Lowell, last
elected President of the United States and the FSE's
puppet. Wild Bill's demise (likewise at the hands of the
Guardians) had not ended that alignment either. Instead
of moving in occupation forces, as they'd done even to
loyal servants such as Dex White, the Effsees had with a
sigh of relief permitted Smith to rule his dominion in
their name and with his own muscle. In fact the Guardians had received reports the Effsees had sent him ar-
maments. Whether or not that was true, the Bible Belt
was a giant red spot as far as the Guardians were concerned. They would steer well clear of it . . . this trip.

The journey was uneventful. They passed innumerable
scenes of devastation and destruction wrought by the
war—or since—and scarcely noticed anymore; they'd
long since become acclimated. But they also passed
fields of grain rippling in the sunshine like gold seas;
herds of grazing cattle; towns where people went about
the daily business of living, on foot, bicycles, horseback, battered vehicles run on the alcohol fuel that had
become the staple of the post-holocaust economy—
signs that made even pessimistic Sam Sloan admit that
life did go on. Slowly, agonizingly, the country was setting foot on the long road to recovery.

As a matter of fact the Guardians' present mission

might just help them on their way. One of their objectives in this California junket was to hook up once again with the enigmatic Dr. Jacob Morgenstern, an architect of the Blueprint for Renewal. Reassembling the scattered pieces of the Blueprint—a top-secret project intended to speed America's reconstruction in the wake of the Third World War—was still the Guardians' primary mission as a team. It was to wrest away as much as possible of the technology and expertise that comprised the Blueprint that the Effsees had invaded in the first place.

Immediately following the war Morgenstern had set about putting together his own one-man reclamation project in California, and he'd made a surprising degree of progress by the time the Guardians first reached the state a year ago. When the Effsees came they had torn apart much of the trade network he'd built; but he had simply gone underground and continued to promulgate both free trade and resistance to the invaders. Through the contacts the Guardians kept with friends and allies in California he had even hinted circumspectly that he'd trolled in a few more Blueprint people if the Guardians cared to come collect them. So the Guardians would be doing their part to help America get back on its feet.

The fact that people tended to scatter in terror at the sight of the diesel-snorting armored car, though, gave clear indication that life was a long shot from being back to normal.

There were others. In Ohio they passed long lines of refugees, trudging by the road with their pitiful possessions humped into bundles on their backs—like the homeless hordes the Guardians had seen in the wake of the war, but with much less to carry. The Guardians speculated on the cause of their plight—plague, disaster, war—but didn't so much as slow down to ask. They had a pressing mission, and since they couldn't help these sufferers, by unspoken consensus they preferred not to know what they were suffering from. They could care when the Effsees were dealt with, not before.

A high-wing propeller plane circled them twice in eastern Nebraska about fifty klicks past the scatter of craters where Omaha used to be, just at dusk. Casey, holding down the Electronic System Operator's seat on that shift, couldn't pick up any traffic from the plane on their computer-driven radio-frequency scanner, but they assumed they had been scoped, and kept driving through the night instead of laagering in for a rest.

In the wee morning hours they came upon a roadblock of highway patrol cars parked nose-to-nose across both the east and westbound lanes of 80. Tom Rogers braked the big car to a stop fifty meters short of the barricade while McKay spiked them with the gigantic spotlight mounted beside the one-man turret. Brave, foolish, or all of the above, the blockaders refused Tom's soft-voiced request for them to clear the road.

The ten metric tons of Mobile One were traveling upwards of eighty klicks an hour when the V-450 hit the juncture of the two cars and spun them aside like Tonka toys kicked by a Godzilla-sized brat. McKay wheeled the turret and hosed tracers from the big Browning .50-caliber after the defenders as they fled into the brush.

"Why are you shooting at them?" Sloan demanded in outrage from the ESO seat.

"They fucking scratched the paint."

Several times during the journey they spotted groups of armed men on horseback; one in Wyoming's Rattlesnake Hills was at least fifty strong. None of them seemed overly interested in a historical reenactment of panzers versus Polish cavalry, so the Guardians passed them by.

"They gotta be up to something," McKay remarked, watching the dust cloud raised by the big troop dwindle in the red and tawny hills behind them out the rear viewport of the V-450.

"There's a lot going on in America we don't know about," Tom said from the turret.

"Yeah," McKay said, turning away. "And sooner or later we're gonna have to find out just what it is."

"If I'm on drugs," Billy McKay said, leaning forward on the wheel of Mobile One, which he'd braked to a stop on a bend in a road winding into the Sierra Nevada north of Death Valley, "why don't I feel better?"

"You're not hallucinating, McKay," Sloan said from the turret. "That's a covered wagon, all right. A genuine prairie schooner, by the looks of it."

Not quite. As it trundled down between the pine-clad slopes of the valley they could see that its wheels were automobile tires. To either side of the driver's box were mounted what looked like whip antennas. From one fluttered a miniature American flag. On the other was a blue-and-gold pennant sporting the block letters UCLA. But other than that, it bore a striking resemblance to the covered wagons of a century and a half before, from the big bowed canvas shell *womping* softly in the breeze, to a team of mules and the grizzle-bearded man with the gray bell-crown top hat and the suspenders stretched across his expanse of belly, sitting up in the high box straining at the brake lever.

He finally got the anachronistic vehicle to squeak to a stop twenty meters shy of the armored car. "Afternoon, gentlemen," he said, doffing his hat to reveal a balding head fringed with long, lank hair. The mules stood with their long ears aimed skeptically at the V-450, which was making little cricket sounds as its titanium-and-steel carapace cooled. The sun was still relatively high in the sky, but the mountains' blue bulk stood between it and the travelers.

"Afternoon." McKay was standing up on the seat, halfway out the top hatch with his big forearms resting on the car's frontal glacis.

"Good afternoon," he heard from behind him. He craned his neck to see Sloan standing up in the turret hatch with his hands in plain sight—not resting on the butterfly triggers of the big automatic weapons.

"Trusting sonofabitch, aren't you?" he subvocalized.

"Come off it, McKay. It's a covered wagon."

The man mopped sweat gloss from his forehead with a blue handkerchief. "Bukowski's the name, Bill Bukowski. I trade in the finest after-the-holocaust luxuries and necessities."

"I'm Billy McKay. This is Sam Sloan. We're the Guardians."

The man rubbed his hairy cheeks with his hankie, put his hat back on, and nodded judiciously. "Thought you might be."

McKay blinked. "I beg your pardon?" Sloan said.

"For one thing, you got the American flag painted on your car," Bukowski said, nodding to the palm-sized insignia painted on the frontal armor next to the ESO's viewport. "Effsees don't usually have that. Also, there's the little matter that you match the descriptions the military government's got plastered on every third telephone pole, offering rewards for information leading to your arrest should you ever set forth in our fair state again."

He tucked the hankie away in a breast pocket of his pink shirt with fake mother-of-pearl snaps and fingered his chin appraisingly. "Offer a pretty penny for you, too. Not just scrip, but gold. Mighty attractive in hard times like these."

The Guardians went tense. *What am I worrying about an old fuck in a Conestoga for?* McKay was asking himself, when Bukowski called, "It's okay, Lynn, they're our kind of people," and the curtain behind him parted and out came a beautiful little Chinese piece with a braided leather band around her head and shouldering a fully-prepped Armbrust antitank rocket launcher that could pop Mobile One's armor like a zit.

CHAPTER
FIVE ─────────────

"Holy shit," Sam breathed.

"Good afternoon, gentlemen," she said in a Southern California accent as pure as Casey's as she settled herself at Bukowski's side. Her teeth were perfect, as white as her long, straight hair was black. She was recapping the Armbrust without bothering to look what she was doing. She'd apparently done it before.

"Gentlemen, permit me to introduce Lynn Pao, my apprentice."

"Pleased to make your acquaintance, Ms. Pao," Sloan said.

"For sure."

"Uh, right," McKay said, fumbling in his pocket for a cigar. "Well, I guess we'll be moving right along now . . ."

"Why don't we set for a spell and palaver," Bill Bukowski said. "Some things you might like to know before moseying up this road."

" 'Palaver'?" McKay repeated. " 'Palaver'?"

"Like, don't mind him," Lynn Pao said. "He's crazy for Western movies. This whole thing is like, y'know, one big wish-fulfillment fantasy for him."

"I'd never know we were almost back in California," McKay said as he dropped back down to his seat.

"Why's that, Billy?" Casey asked.

"Never mind."

McKay turned the car round and rolled back down a hundred meters to a place where a leveled-off pulloff for a scenic overlook allowed Bukowski to park his wagon.

"God, what beautiful country," Sam Sloan said, clambering from the turret to drop down to the gravel with a crunch. He stood, threw his head back and his chest out, stretched his arms to their full extension, and filled his lungs with crisp, resin-tinged air. "I feel like I could run ten miles."

"Don't even think about it, Sam," Tom said seriously. "Altitude sickness."

While Sam was still shaking his head and clucking over the team medic's literal-mindedness, McKay emerged from the vehicle. He straightened, took a cigar from a pocket of his green-and-brown cammie coveralls, began to remove the crinkly plastic wrapper.

" 'Scenic Overlook,' huh," he read from the arrowhead-shaped sign by the turnoff. He stuck the cigar in his face, lit it, and stood staring out east across the Great Basin. The mountains' shadow flowed out into it like a dark sea; beyond, the land was all tawny and pink and grayish-green, broken by hogbacks and abrupt mesas like red-flanked icebergs, while cloud shadows drifted across it like rudderless ships.

McKay shook his head. "Dunno what's so scenic about it. Looks like a whole lotta nothin' to me."

"How can you be that insensitive to the beauty of this land, McKay?" Sam wailed in outrage.

"Only thing country like this is good for is making beer commercials," McKay said, and turned away to watch Bukowski's apprentice stretching up to check some kind of rigging on the wagon's white hood. The motion tautened the faded fabric of her jeans in a real interesting way, and he reflected that this Ms. Pao sure had a good class of ass.

Lynn Pao let the mules graze on the scruffy grass by the verge. Bukowski dropped the tailgate of the wagon and cranked some coffee beans through the hand mill he had mounted in the back. He claimed the beans were from Colombia, imported since the war. The Guardians were skeptical, but Casey heated water in Mobile One's microwave and when the coffee was ready, Sam, who was a coffee snob, opined that it was indeed the real thing, and fresh. McKay shrugged; coffee was coffee to him, whether it came from Colombia or the International House of Pancakes.

"Quite a haul across those mountains," Sam observed, sipping.

Bukowski shrugged. "Sight better'n in the old days, before they ever heard of paved roads. Still, it wasn't much fun, I don't mind telling you."

"What brings you across the Sierras, Mr. Bukowski?" Casey asked, smiling at Lynn Pao. She smiled back.

McKay wanted to throttle him. He already *had* a woman in California, dammit. But he just seemed to attract them, wherever they went.

"Effsees. Got to be too much trouble doing business in the state. Thought I'd move on for a spell, until things settled down."

"What kind of trouble?" McKay asked.

"Rationing. Regulation. That kinda shit. Make you take out twelve kind of licenses before you can sell a pair of underwear. Now, don't get me wrong, we got a healthy, thriving black market in the late, great state of California, but that's hardly a suitable occupation for a party who works out of a mule-drawn wagon and is too old and fat to run fast."

Far from being old and fat, Bukowski looked fiftyish and was built along the lines of a cinnamon bear, low to the ground and heavy in the belly; but solid, serviceable. His assistant laughed and ruffled his beard.

"Old Jake'll cuss me up one side and down the other for bugging out," the trader went on, "but there's the practicalities—"

"I beg your pardon," Sam said, "but who did you say?"

"Old Jake. Jacob Morgenstern. Economist, Israeli fella, used to be a paratrooper. Thought you boys knew him."

"We do," Sloan said. "We were just surprised you did."

"Know him? Shoot. Helped me get my wagon built. Helps all kind of people get started in various kinds of business . . . Effsees got a price on his head, of course."

It was approaching evening, so the Guardians sluiced water for the mules from the V-450's tank into a couple of Bukowski's buckets and invited the trader and his assistant to dinner.

"Say, this is really excellent tofu," Lynn Pao enthused. They were all sitting on the gravel next to the wagon to eat. "You wouldn't think freeze-dried would taste so, y'know, natural."

McKay fought the impulse to gag. They had foisted off on the vegetarian Ms. Pao one of the special meal packets they'd captured with the car back in Heartland, which even Casey couldn't stomach. Aside from the fact that McKay hated the very *idea* of tofu, and the thought of freeze-dried tofu made his guts churn like a washing machine out of control, it reminded him of the mystery of just whom the armored car had been waiting for, that frenetic morning in the middle of summer.

"Mentioned something earlier 'bout us not wanting to use this road, Mr. Bukowski," Tom said.

"That I did, Mr. Rogers. There's an Effsee roadblock just on the California side of the pass."

McKay slit-eyed him across his spaghetti. "How'd you get across?"

Bukowski laughed. "Not all the Effsees are hard-asses. Lot of 'em are good American boys—or British, or French, or German—just lookin' to get by." He reached up behind him under the driver's box, produced a videocassette in a faded glorious-colored jacket. "Made 'em a little deal, gave them a few of these to open the road for a couple of minutes."

McKay took the box and studied it. *"Seka's Midnight Fantasies.* Good God, this is a priceless cultural resource."

"And where might we find this roadblock, Mr. Bukowski?" Tom asked gently.

"You boys got a map?"

The Guardians did indeed have a map. Casey carefully collected the foil trays from the meal, carried them over, and dumped them into a rusting fifty-five gallon oil drum welded to a chain, which was welded to a steel post sunk in cement. Then he caught McKay looking at him very hard, and blushed.

"If you'll just step into the vehicle, Mr. Bukowski," McKay said, "—and your charming assistant—we'll take a look at our map." Ms. Pao smiled. Sam rolled his eyes.

"You think it's a good idea to let them into our vehicle?" he subvocalized as McKay helped hand Lynn into the V-450.

For a moment McKay fought the magnetic force drawing his hand irresistibly to the gorgeous curve of the apprentice's ass, and then turned to his buddy. "What, you think he's got a charge of C-4 strapped to his chest, or just a microcamera hidden in one of them fancy buttons? You just don't trust him 'cause he's a capitalist."

"He's a self-confessed black marketeer."

"Like I said. And just what do you think that makes Dr. Jake Morgenstern?"

Casey had the nav display up on the screen between the driver's and ESO's seats when McKay and Sloan climbed into the hot gloom of the car. The supercomputer built into the vehicle had a complete set of U.S. Geological Survey maps hardwired into ROM, with your choice of scale from 1/24,000 on up. Lynn Pao cooed admiringly while Bukowski stood by with his fingers scrabbling like small clumsy animals in his beard, a skeptical frown folding his forehead.

"All right," Casey said, scrolling the map with the trackball mounted on the console; he loved this shit, it reminded him of video games, his one addiction, as dear to his heart as beer and cigars to McKay's. "Here we are, right under the cursor. Now I'll, like, take us back up the road . . . you think you can pick out where this roadblock is, Mr. Bukowski, or—?"

"I can read a map, son. It should be—hold it, hold it right there." A spatulate finger stabbed down. "Should be about here. But something about this doesn't look right. I think your map's a bit off."

"It's the finest map available, compiled by the United States Government," Sloan all but sniffed.

"Yeah. Same folks managed to get us into this fix, with folks ridin' around on horseback and bartering for the basics of life. Not that I'm complainin' myself. Lynn's right; I really get into this. Beats the fanny off lawyering."

"Uh, well," Sam said. "But you feel it's here, right after this bend?"

"Not altogether. But it's as close as this map'll show, I reckon."

Sam pecked at the computer keyboard, entering the roadblock's putative location in memory. The others stepped back outside.

The sun had sunk most of the way behind the Sierras, now, turning all the broad land dusty purple except for a mountain range glowing like a band of gold across the horizon. "God, I love this country," Bukowski said. "Tough to make a living out of, though. I wish you boys the best of luck in kicking the Effsees into the Pacific."

Three pairs of eyes fastened immovably on him. "Uh, exactly what do you mean by that, Mr. Bukowski?" Tom asked. McKay had the distinct impression his right hand was gravitating toward the leaf-bladed Gerber Mark II combat knife that hung hilt-downward across the left breast of his cammies. The one he used for silent killing—for fighting he used the beefy Bowie-style Kabar at his hip.

"Like, everybody in the state is wondering when you were, y'know, gonna come back and do something about the Effsees," Lynn Pao said. "The way you took care of crazy Geoff van Damm was pretty awesome. We knew you'd be back to help."

"Fuck me," McKay said.

"Don't you wish," Sloan subvocalized from the door behind him. "Looks like we're heroes in these parts."

McKay winced and took out a fresh cigar—or at least a new one; the cigars scavenged from urban ruins were a bit past the fresh stage. His throat was dry. Hell, he knew they were heroes all along—but still, it was a hell of a billing to live up to.

"Have a cigar on me, son. Grown since the war. Not turned to plasterboard like that plastic-wrapped thing you got."

"Yeah? Where'd it come from?"

"Indonesia," said Lynn Pao.

"In-do-*ne*-sia?" He took the cigar Bukowski was proferring. It was black and hard as an aged dog turd. He sniffed it dubiously. His eyebrows rose. Bukowski scratched a match alight on the buckle of his suspenders and lit it for him.

"Say, this ain't half-bad," McKay said, surprised.

"Have a box. But I got something to ask in return, son."

"What?" McKay asked, squinting suspiciously through aromatic smoke.

"I reckon the Effsees won't be quite as willing to let that big old battlewagon in as they were to let us out. And I figure you got your own ways of persuading them." Bukowski let his eyes drift up to the stubby automatic grenade launcher and the longer barrel of the big machine gun mounted next to it.

"I reckon we do," Sam Sloan said. He couldn't help warming to this old dude, McKay noticed; capitalist or not, he gave Sloan the chance to play thank-God-I'm-a-country-boy.

Bukowski nodded slowly. "Then I'd be obliged if you'd wait till a bit after midnight to bust the road-block. Boys let me through are good boys, American boys, and they ain't too happy with what they're doin', even though they think it's their duty. They're good people; dealt with their kind every day, back inside."

"You traded with en—with the Federated States forces?" Sloan asked.

Bukowski grinned a slow grin and lit an Indonesian rope of his own. "You bet I did. I'm a businessman, Lieutenant Sloan. Fact is, I was an official sutler, fully licensed and accredited to trade with the expeditionary force. Made a pretty penny at it, before I got fed up."

"Anything for a buck, huh?" Sloan said.

"Yep," Bukowski said. "And for nice new military equipment like that tankbuster my little sweetheart here was fixing to use in case you turned out to be the wrong sort of people. And dispositions and relief schedules for Effsee garrisons all over the state. And maybe a teeny weeny bit of advance notice when the Effsees were gonna raid a settlement suspected of aiding the resistance." He shrugged. "But I finally reached my limit, and now I'm headed for Reno to see how business is there."

He ambled over to check the harnesses of the mules, slap them affectionately on their muscular necks. "Anyway, I'd appreciate if you'd wait to go through, like I asked. Boys who let me through get relieved at midnight."

"You got it," McKay said.

CHAPTER
SIX

"Holy shit," Casey yelped.

Standing behind him and Sloan, McKay just had time to be startled at the language—Casey almost never cussed—before he had to catch himself to keep from taking a nose dive into the nav screen as Casey rammed down the brake pedal. The big car wallowed like a tugboat in high seas, then went chugging back around the curve in the road as fast as it had come.

"Just what the fuck was that about?" McKay demanded as the car slowed to a saner stop. The lights of the console display, which were the compartment's only illumination, lent his face a bizarre look. "I almost left my goddam teeth in the back of Sloan's seat."

"Roadblock, Billy," Tom said over the intercom from the turret.

"Dammit, it wasn't supposed to be for half a klick!"

"I told you we couldn't trust the man," Sloan said.

"No, Sam, look at this." Casey was hunched over the

map screen. "He was right. Map's off—bend we just took isn't on it at all. I think Mr. Bukowski picked the place that looked most like what he remembered, man."

"Fuckin' far out," McKay snarled, ripping his Maremont from the clips that held it flush with the hull by the door, preparatory to bailing out. "The Effsees gonna be all over us like crabs on a five-dollar whore in about ten seconds." The car had been running slow with IR lamps only for illumination, but the force manning the roadblock had to have heard the engine in this still mountain air.

"Hold up, McKay." Sloan was punching buttons in rapid sequence. "Their transmitter's hot, but they're not broadcasting yet. Here—it's electronic-warfare time."

He hit another button and sat back with a smug expression. "Jamming. Unless they have a semi tractor set up to run their generator they won't punch a signal through that. They won't let their friends know we're here just yet."

Casey was doing some button-punching of his own. A blare of white noise erupted from speakers set into the console. Casey winced and turned down the gain. The white-noise rush resolved into a magnified torrent of forest sounds: the soft breeze roaring like a cataract; pine needles clashing like giant insect mandibles; twigs clattering like a load of wooden crates being driven down a washboard road; all picked up by the hull-mounted shotgun mike Casey had swung to bear on the roadblock, now out of sight around the bend. As the former fighter pilot worked, computer filters peeled back layer after layer of noise, until voices broke abruptly into the cabin, agitated and loud.

Casey frowned. "Damn. They're speaking French."

"I know French," McKay said; just something he'd

picked up with Force RECON and SOG-SWAC in the Southern Med, where French was almost as universal as Arabic and a damned sight easier to learn. He was poised with the pig in one hand and the door latch in the other, listening.

"What do they say?" Casey asked.

"They're arguing about what they saw," translated Sloan, who also spoke French and hated to be shown up by McKay. "No one's gotten around to coming to investigate just yet."

"Hit up the low light," McKay directed.

Casey had reflexively switched off the infrared beams when they ditched back around the corner; no reason in the world to believe the Effsee team wouldn't have night-vision devices like IR goggles. There were low-light TV cameras mounted in Mobile One's bow and turret. They gave pictures like kinescopes of old fifties black-and-white television shows, but were good enough to see anybody coming down the road and might even show someone sneaking through the woods, if anybody got that bold.

"Anybody see what they got?" McKay asked when Casey had followed his order.

"Looked like a big log across the road and a vehicle behind, just like Mr. Bukowski said," Casey said.

"I think the vehicle's a hummer, Billy," supplied Rogers.

"Great." A combat vehicle like an outsized, lightly armored jeep, a hummer could carry quite a sting, up to and including pop-up launchers for TOW or Hellfire antitank missiles meant to take out much tougher targets than Mobile One.

"Bukowski thought they kept maybe a squad up here," Sam said.

"I like this," McKay said. "Do they patrol every goddam goat track in these hills?''

"I think we just got lucky, Billy," Casey said.

"Yeah. Well, our buddies are starting to wonder why they're just getting noise on their radio, so we got to do something smart and quick. Tom, get your quiet piece and come with me. Sloan, shinny up into the turret and take over for him. You and Case be ready to come running if we holler.''

Rogers hit the catch on a compartment set in the hull and took out a submachine gun with the fat shroud of an integral silencer swelling the barrel. He paused to collect a cordura pouch of grenades and followed McKay into the night.

It was a fine night for snooping and pooping. A few high clouds floated among the stars, and the moon was only a promising glow from behind the peaks to the east. For all the lowlands' heat the air was sharp, foretelling the snow that would seal the little two-lane road in a matter of weeks.

McKay went high and right onto the wooded rising slope, Rogers low and left into the trees that now blocked the roadblock from view. McKay worked his way well up into the trees, making his way with a silence that was highly unusual for a very large man carrying a four-foot chunk of iron that tipped the scale at twenty pounds. He was taking his time, relying on Sloan to warn him if the situation suddenly got immediate. No matter how much fun McKay had ragging Sloan's ass he trusted him implicitly.

Though Rogers's route led through undergrowth McKay wasn't afraid the ex–Green Beret would make any noises the chattering French soldiers could detect. He was convinced the man could walk across a ballroom floor littered with dry leaves and not make a sound.

The roadblock was sited less than a kilometer from

the head of the pass. Angling downward toward the road McKay finally got a look at it. It was pretty much as advertised, a stout log winched across the road, rifle pits dug for the troopies in the shoulder to either side of the pavement. Several men armed with these funky MAS rifles, which always reminded him of clarinet cases with carrying handles, were standing in the road in front of the log and peering off at the bend, debating the significance of the peculiar event of perhaps five minutes ago. Clearly they thought it was either not disturbing enough to go check out, or else too disturbing to go check out. They were not expecting trouble, out here on this obscure road up to hell and gone in the mountains. But neither were they too eager to go hunting for it.

Back in the scrub oak across the road from where McKay was easing himself down and lowering the bipod of his machine gun a hummer was parked with a couple more soldiers in berets and cammie smocks standing behind it, craning to look down the road. A third man swore at the vehicle's radio, and a kerosene lantern set on the ground at their feet illuminated anxious faces. The long barrel of a .50-caliber in a ring mount poked out over their heads.

There were a few nylon-mesh lawn chairs arranged in a sort of circle around the lantern, and a TV tray lay on its side in the middle of them. Obviously Mobile One's arrival had interrupted a nocturnal card game. Equally obviously, the soldiers clearly weren't expecting any company. Which was just as well—in the rifle pit on his side of the road he saw the distinctive streamlined spermatozoa shape of an RPG-7V antitank rocket. Had the Frogs been alert they could have made the Guardians' lives both miserable and brief.

"Billy, I'm in position," Tom's voice said in his ear.

He started to respond, but then came Sloan's voice: "McKay, I think they've spotted you."

McKay froze. The dudes out front of the big log were now staring up directly at him, one of them looking like something from a John Carpenter flick with an alien-eye set of starlight binoculars distorting his face.

"Well, shit," McKay said. "Fire 'em up, Tom."

Before he'd finished forming the words deep in his throat he saw two of the men back by the truck crumple as Roger caught them with a silenced burst from his MP-5—and it was virtually silent, firing big, fat, sub-sonic .45 rounds. But it was too late for stealth, thanks to some sonofabitch having the presence of mind to scope the slopes overlooking his position.

McKay yanked the pin on a grenade and lobbed it. It bounced once and went off about ten feet in front of the men before the barricade with a tremendous white flash and a head-splitting crack. The man with the fancy binocs let out a yelp and went staggering back, blinded.

His buddies were standing there blinking with their jawbones dangling—the concussion grenade didn't need the help of light-enhancement gear to dazzle you. McKay settled himself behind the Maremont and chopped them both down with a single quick burst.

The M-60's enormous muzzle flash got everybody's attention right away. Answering fire flamed from the rifle pits. McKay felt grit sting his cheek from near-misses, and these long three-prong ponderosa needles were showering around him, kicked up by the storm of jacketed lead. *These fuckers are more on the ball than I thought.*

White light erupted from the rifle pit on the far side of the road as if a volcano had fired up inside it; fragments of phosphorus from Tom's grenade, burning hot enough to melt steel, stuck to the occupants' hands and

faces and clothing and ate in. Burning, howling figures
scrambled out of the pit, demon figures wreathed in
dense poisonous white smoke. McKay put them out of
their misery—his 7.62-millimeter slugs hit faster than
heroin, and gave much-longer-lasting relief.

The big fifty mounted on the hummer cut loose with a
roar that shook the mountainside. It seemed to McKay
that he could feel the heat of the muzzle flash, and at
this close range the shock waves of the cartridges going
off jackhammered him, dynamic overpressure making it
hard to breathe. Huge white splinters were knocked out
of the boles of trees, limbs came crashing down, im-
mense divots of earth went flying everywhere. Being on
the receiving end of .50-caliber fire was nothing like fun
at the best of times. When you weren't forty meters
from the gun, it was like being a stationary clay pigeon
at a skeet-shooting championship, with all the best
special effects from an earthquake, a hailstorm, and an
electrical storm thrown in.

McKay had several options, none of them good. He
could shoot it out, try to bug out, mix it up dodging and
shooting. There was also prayer. McKay opted to stay
where he was and hose tracer desperately into the hummer; though it lacked the awesome smashing power of
the fifty-cal, the Maremont had enough punch at this
range to have a good chance of defeating the vehicle's
thin armor. The fifty-gunner was chewing up the hillside
pretty much at random, so McKay had as much chance
of stopping a round trying to get clear as he did hanging
in where he lay—not that he'd actually stop one of the
half-ounce slugs; at this range they'd pretty much turn
you inside out and hardly even slow down. And prayer
was out; he was the next best thing to an atheist.

He kept pouring rounds into the hummer as fast as
the 60 would cycle them, barely coming off the trigger

to break up the burst and minimize the risk of a jam.
There'd been fifty rounds on the belt coiled inside the
plastic half-moon ammo box hung on the machine gun's
receiver, and whatever was left he was giving to the vehicle and thinking, *Fuck me, he can't go on missing forever.*

Snorting like a dragon, Mobile One came bombing
around the bend. Its big searchlight stabbed out like a
Martian deathray, hunted a millisecond, pinned the
hummer with white-hot radiance as the V-450 rocked to
a stop with its angular snout a handsbreadth from the
log across the road. The .50-caliber could quite possibly
have penetrated Mobile One's armor, especially if it was
firing armor-piercers, but whether startled, dazzled, or
just generally freaked, the hummer's gunner swung his
piece blindly around, spewing yellow tracers in a long
arc up the mountainside.

Sam Sloan never gave him the fractional second he
needed to get his act together. Both Mobile One's turret
guns cut loose in a syncopated duet. McKay saw the
hummer heel way over on its suspension under the
sledgehammer impacts of .50-caliber rounds and 40-
millimeter grenades. Then a wave of orange-white flame
washed it out of his vision.

He buried his face in the soft pine-needle mat and the
crumbly dark soil beneath as assorted spare parts and
cooked-off rounds pelted down around him. His head
felt as if a blacksmith had laid it on his anvil and been
whanging at it with a hammer. The fight hadn't lasted
long, but it had sure been loud.

When the hummer's explosion calmed down a bit he
dared to raise his head. The roadblock's survivors had
long since vanished into the brush. Casey had the hatch
popped and was standing up out of it admiring his
handiwork.

"I know you didn't call us, Billy," he called up when he saw his leader's face, blackened with burned powder and with little clumps of earth dropping off it, poke up out of a bush. "But when we heard the big gun cut loose we thought maybe we shouldn't wait. You aren't like, mad at us?"

"I'll forgive you this time." McKay noticed that his voice sounded as if it came from very, very far away. He picked himself up and cupped his hands around his mouth.

"Listen up, boys," he called to the woods and the night in his rude, slangy French. "Tell your friends the Guardians are back.

"And this time we're here to stay!"

CHAPTER
SEVEN ————————————————

Bonnie Sanchez was built like a brick shithouse —big and solid and square, though she didn't have a peaked roof. She had a round face and round nose and black eyes behind round glasses, and though she must have been in her early twenties she wore her black hair in pigtails. She had on a gray T-shirt beneath worn blue overalls. As she spoke with the Guardians she turned a ten-inch plastic toy robot over in her hands, the kind that folds up to resemble something else. One of its blocky arms had come off. She turned it this way and that, flexing it, feeling it, seeming almost to read it like a blind person reading a page of braille.

"You missed the big news," she said.

Suddenly she frowned, held the robot an inch in front of her nose, then took it to arm's length, up in a shaft of sunlight slanting down through redwood beams from the clerestory of the big central living-and-working room. "Hey, all right, give me a hot knife, some wire, and some needle-nose pliers, and I can fix this sucker good as new. Better. They made these things cheap.''

Seated on heavy wood-block furniture and cushions upholstered in the gray and black and earth-tone stripes and geometric patterns of Navajo rugs, the Guardians gave each other glassy eyeballs. Somewhere in the background a cassette machine played old Police; Casey was absently tapping the wing of his shooting glasses on his knee in time to Sting.

"Julio'll be happy to hear that," said another one of their hosts, a man of indeterminate youth named Charles, with a dirty GI T-shirt and jeans, brown hair lying like an untied knot atop his head, a few strands of beard and mustache wisping off his face, and a spare-tire roll about the middle of him.

"Julio's one of the neighbor kids, up from Pine-holm," Charles explained to the Guardians. Pineholm was the little town that lay beneath the pine-tipped bluff below the redwood redoubt of Vista Systems, Inc. "They're always bringing stuff by for Bonnie to work on. Not just toys, either; she can fix *anything*."

People were coming and going from the big room, and various of the half dozen or so on hand at the moment made concurring noises. McKay noted that they appeared to come in two sizes: painfully thin and large economy.

Bonnie had picked up a soldering gun off a wooden coffee table that looked as if it had been built expressly to hide under in case of one of California's trademarked earthquakes. Its top was scarred with long black burn marks; whether from aggressive neglect of smoking materials or leaving hot soldering guns lying around on it was not clear. She gave the Guardians a distracted smile as she began fiddling with the gun.

"Ah, excuse me," said Sam at his most diplomatic,

"but I believe you said something about big news."

Bonnie looked up, blinked. "Say what?"

McKay shifted in his chair, said nothing. Better to leave this to Sloan, because this passel of nerds ensconced in their vast red house sprawled on the western face of the Sierra Nevada in the Mother Lode country east of Modesto comprised the Guardians' most valuable allies in California. These were the computer whizzes who, along with the high-tech holdouts of Colorado's Freehold, held the FSE's satellite communications net in the palms of their pudgy hands.

"Big news," Sloan said, his smile showing strain at the corners. "We missed it . . . you said."

"Oh, yeah." She tossed the soldering gun back on the table and took out a yellow felt-tip marker from a pocket of her coveralls and began to play with that. "Well, it seems the Effsees have decided to pull the military government out of Sacramento and head south. Shortening their lines of supply, they call it. I wonder. They can get supplies in through San Francisco Bay as well as through L.A. port or Dago."

"Southern California just naturally attracts fascist types," said a tall, thin, pimpled specimen in a Spiderman T-shirt.

"Hey," said Casey.

"The north just got too hot for them," somebody else offered. "Too much guerrilla—ooh, pardon me, 'terrorist'—activity up here."

"Does this mean they're getting ready to pull out, you think?" Sam asked.

McKay gave him a look. *What do these wimps know about stuff like that?*

"Not just yet," said a narrow blond girl with a long, thin nose and straight, lank hair hanging almost to her waist. "But concentrating their forces makes it easier to withdraw them if they decide the situation in Europe warrants it. Plus it makes it easier for them to keep what they do want to hang on to."

"Right," McKay said sarcastically. Then he thought a moment and said, "Yeah, that *is* right. Son of a bitch."

"Lisa's into that militarist stuff," Charles said. "She thinks Clausewitz is a turn-on."

"Better him than you, Charles."

"This doesn't mean they're letting go of the North entirely," Bonnie said. "They're leaving some troops up here in various places. Garrisons, or whatever you call them."

"Yes, it's garrisons," Lisa said tartly. "*Some* people."

The booming software days of the early eighties, when pimpled high school dropouts with Apples in their bedrooms made overnight fortunes from game design, were history and had been for a decade. But for all the noise the computer explosion had made, it had barely nicked the paint of the field's potential. Ever-increasing hardware speed and capacity, improved architecture, and above all development of interactive software meant that there was still lots of room for the brilliant amateur, the juvenile hacker with the agile mind and boundless need to know how things worked. The first big blush of computer fad had passed—the vidgame craze, the computerized recipe files—but it left the computer demystified, robbed of the ominous presence a generation of fear-peddlers had given it. People began actually to *think* about the magic idiot box, just what it could be used for.

The hardware revolution was over, the software revolution fought out. The applications revolution had only just begun. Vista Systems, Inc., had been established to interface the gifted amateur and the hungry market for sophisticated systems: robotics, expert programs, artificial intelligence. Its founder had inherited a fortune immodest enough to build this combination dorm, lab, and playground up here at the edge of the mountains, and equip it with all the latest goodies. The money gone, the founder had then trolled in thirty or forty talented youngsters with the promise of being able to do what they did best and be appreciated for it—and paid, if things panned out. They did, and everybody here at Chaos Castle had been making great pots of money up until the balloon went up.

The One-Day War had put a quick stop to the money inflow. Yet the postpubescent *wunderkinder* of Chaos Castle had been getting by just fine after the End of the World, thanks to their own ingenuity—and some help from the ubiquitous Dr. Jacob Morgenstern.

"The people here vend their services as tinkers, doing everything from recharging batteries off their solar accumulators to large-scale electrical repair and design," the spare brown man said, sipping coffee Arab-fashion, sweetened to the point a spoon would just about stand in it unaided. "Ms. Sanchez is especially adept at helping to build electrical generators of various sorts, whether powered by sunlight or fuels such as wood, alcohol, or methane, and making whatever adjustments are needed to get them to power tools and appliances —you understand this lies beyond my area of competence, of course."

"Of course, Dr. Morgenstern," said Sam Sloan, in a tone that indicated he didn't believe *anything* really lay outside the area of the older man's competence.

"They do quite a lucrative trade, selling their ex-

pertise all over the state—much of it of a nature quite
unsanctioned by our lords and masters from Europe, as
you're well aware.''

Billy McKay was staring at his coffee mug as though
if he stared at it hard enough it would turn into a can of
Bud. "Why haven't the Effsees poked their snouts in,
then?"

"As a man of your experience ought well to be
aware," Morgenstern said, in English that was more
Oxford-accented than Israeli, for all that he was *sabra*,
"even ten thousand men is no great number to secure an
area as vast as the state of California. Especially one
whose population is so inclined to fractiousness. This
locale is inconveniently placed for them to subject it to
too much scrutiny." He sipped.

McKay sat there with his ears on fire and glowered.
Most men got to talk that way to him about once before
he started twisting their parts off. But Dr. Jacob Morgenstern's person was sacrosanct; he was one of the men
the shadowy Major Crenna had called upon to design
the Blueprint for Renewal back before the war, and
since the war he'd been building up a trade-and-mu-
tual-defense network on which the Guardians had to
rely if they were going to damage the Effsees—a network that would be vital in rebuilding not just the state
but America as a whole, once the Effsees were dealt
with; if they were. He was Maximum Man in these
parts. More than that, he was a former paratrooper
who'd jumped into Mitla Pass with Sharon's 202nd almost half a century before, and he'd commanded a tank
brigade on the Golan Heights in '73, and besides that
was a master of *aikido*, and McKay wasn't any too
damned sure he could do the caustic old fart much
harm, for all that he must have had a hundred pounds
on him.

"Furthermore," the doctor continued, ignoring McKay's expression, "the people here at Vista have done little to attract attention to themselves. They don't deal in black-market commodities—the occupying forces aren't even competent totalitarians, or they'd proscribe consumer electronics before anything—and they themselves don't physically move goods. It's people who transport items who attract the attention."

"One thing I don't understand, Doctor," Sam Sloan said. "These kids here have satellite communications, which entails stuff like antenna dishes. Why haven't the Effsees spotted them from the air?"

"You've been around the grounds some, surely? You've seen the storage sheds, with the plastic temporary roofing? The antennae are concealed in those."

"You sure got here quick, Doctor," Casey Wilson remarked. He was splayed out in a chair with knees and head at the same altitude, looking boneless as a dozing cat. "We haven't been here more than a few hours."

The doctor permitted himself one of his sparse half-smiles. "Times change. I no longer have to rely on my own two feet or a donkey's four for transportation. I use a motorcycle now, with the carburetor adjusted to burn alcohol."

Casey grinned at the image of the dignified doctor putting along the shoulder past the lines of decaying cars that choked California's major roadways, his brown and black and gray *aba* fluttering in the breeze, his hawknosed face, burned to the color and consistency of mahogany by decades of harsh sunlight, thrust forward over the handlebars. Moses on a motorbike, except Morgenstern's gray-ginger beard was more a goatee than the splendid growth Casey usually pictured Moses as possessing.

"And of course my friends here at Vista gave me

ample notice of your impending arrival."

"I understand you've found some more Blueprint participants, Doc . . . tor." Not even McKay could bring himself to call Morgenstern "Doc."

The narrow head nodded. "That's so."

"I suppose you'll be wanting to hand them over to us."

"Not at all," Morgenstern said crisply.

"Why the hell not?"

"Right now your task is to undertake a campaign to convince Chairman Maximov his expeditionary force would do him far more good helping defend him from Islamist fanatics than being nibbled to death far away in the wilderness of America. The Blueprint personnel are in a reasonably secure location, more secure than any you might now provide. And the fact that you'll be engaged in hostile activity against the occupiers raises the unfortunate possibility you might be captured. It's imperative that these people do not fall into the hands of the FSE, Lieutenant McKay."

McKay scowled and worked his big jaw around as though trying to chew up a piece of shoe leather. Reflex told him to make a lot of macho noises about how the pukes'd never break *him*, but the seasoned soldier and former SOG-SWAC dirty-warfare artist he was knew better than that. The Effsees had drugs that would make him reel off everything he knew like a tape recorder.

"Yeah," he admitted, as if the word hurt his gut, which it did. "You're right."

"When you can arrange safe transport back to Washington for them, I shall hand them over. Not before."

Briefly he frowned. "I wish I could go myself. The thought of Marguerite Connolly—" He shook his head. "But I should speak no ill of a colleague—especially inasmuch as I myself approved her inclusion in the Blue-print."

"Say all you want, Doctor," McKay said with feel-ing. But the doctor pushed himself up from his chair with an agility that belied his age and went off to work out on the terrace.

CHAPTER
EIGHT ——————————————

"So what's happenin', dudes?" asked the black man with the shaven head and the mirror shades.

"Idaho! Far *out!*" Casey shouted. He ran to embrace him, then reached over his muscular shoulder to grasp hands with the lean white dude in shorts and soccer shirt who stood behind him. "Lancelot! How's life been treating you, man?"

"Shitty," Lancelot said. "Fascist Effsees are, like, everywhere. It's getting so even the back roads aren't safe anymore."

He cast his eyes nervously around the lantern-lit San Ramon lounge and ran a hand through his long, wavy blond hair. "I don't even know what we're doing here, man. We're never gonna be able to do anything about the Effsees. They're just too fuckin' strong, I tell you."

"Hey, Lancelot, like, lighten up," Idaho said, letting go of Casey.

Lancelot dropped his eyes, raised them again. "Sorry."

"I can see our strategy session's getting off to a helluva start," McKay said sourly around the butt of his cigar. He caught one of the skinny-type Vista Systems people rolling his eyes at him and then up at a poster he'd tacked on the wall, that showed a dragon and the legend: "NO SMOKING; VIOLATORS WILL BE EATEN."

"Don't hassle me, Jack, I ain't lighting it," he said, marveling a little at the balls these nerds had, to march in here and stick up their damn signs as if they owned the place. "I need all the reassurance I can get just now."

He shook hands with Idaho. "Good to see you, dude. And you Lance. How . . . forget I said that."

Dr. Morgenstern had set up a meeting between the Guardians and representatives of his network for the day after their arrival at Chaos Castle in an insignificant town called San Ramon, about thirty klicks from Pineholm—far enough, he judged, to reduce the risk of compromising the invaluable Vista Systems to an acceptable level. Like everybody else in California, it seemed, the proprietor of this flyspeck-and-tinsel cantina knew the Israeli economist. He or one of his hirelings stood polishing glasses beneath a neon Coors sign that hadn't been lit since the One-Day War—that showed you how out-of-the-way San Ramon was, a California bar that advertised Coors—looking like a slimmed-down chipmunk with an apron and a neatly kept full-face beard. He was obviously keeping lookout that the peculiar crew assembling among the round-topped tables didn't start busting the place up.

It wasn't all that unlikely. Jacob Morgenstern had some kind of social theory he'd discussed till late last night with Sam Sloan, a discussion which had sent Billy McKay to bed early for some much-needed rest. From what he'd caught of the conversation, he gathered that the doctor figured that a society worked better the fewer rules it laid down, that the best way for people to get along was for them to pretty much go off and do what they wanted, with the one ground rule being that they minded their own business and didn't go interfering with their neighbors. McKay wasn't real sure how well a setup like that would work. On the other hand, he basically believed in minding his own business, and had bounced his knuckles off snouts which people were trying to stick into his business more times than he could easily call to mind, so maybe the doc had something, at that.

Whether because of his Theory of Minimal Consensus or from sheer necessity, since the FSE invasion Morgenstern had been cobbling together a coalition out of elements with nothing more in common than a hard-on for the Effsee military government. There were a few familiar faces among the crowd—Idaho and Lancelot, of course. But also there were Lori and Donna, the lesbian sea gypsies who'd given the Guardians a lift to L.A. last year when they had been hunting former Lieutenant Governor Geoff van Damm, his Japanese Red Army bodyguards, and his recommissioned hydrogen bomb to ground in Disneyland. Most were unfamiliar however, and some were clenched with suspicion, eyes moving restlessly, harsh and unfriendly. There were some former and current enemies under this roof.

"So how's Rhoda?" Casey asked Idaho and Lancelot.

Their eyes moved away from Casey's. "Uh, well, she's getting by, like," Lancelot mumbled.

"Hey, wait, has something happened to her? What's the matter?"

But Morgenstern was rapping hardwood knuckles on a tabletop, calling the meeting to order.

In a few moments the chatter grumbled down into silence and people found chairs. Outside was late afternoon, but here it was murky twilight that only a half dozen lanterns and an open door saved from pitch blackness. Nothing much could be done about the heat of the day or the more than a score of bodies crammed in between the black-velvet paintings on the walls.

"Ladies, gentlemen, we are about to open a new phase of our campaign against the invaders from the Federated States of Europe," Morgenstern announced, standing in front of the postage-stamp bandstand.

"It's about time," shouted a young man from the back. He was middle height and wiry, with lean features and a fleshy nose and curly black hair, and the sort of intense manner McKay for some reason associated with bicycle racers.

"I know that many of you have hungered to take the offensive against the Expeditionary Force. Now you shall have your wish—in a very limited way, Mr. Duvall." The bike racer crossed his arms defiantly over his chest. "It would behoove you, all of you, to keep in mind that taking a more aggressive stance will be extremely dangerous. Battle is not all the clean, clear-cut heroics you see in the movies."

"Life since the One-Day War hasn't exactly been a picnic, Doctor," remarked a young woman sitting up front. McKay couldn't see her well from where he stood, back toward the bar, but remembered from seeing her before that she was on the stocky, squat side, with short hair and a hint of mustache.

"Quite so, Ms. Gambatelli. Now, before we discuss our plan of action, I'd like to introduce the men who will be directing the campaign in the field. Some of you may have heard of them. They're a special team known as the Guardians: Thomas Rogers, Samuel Sloan, Kenneth C. Wilson, and their leader, William Kosciusko McKay. Lieutenant McKay, if you'd care to say a few words?"

Each Guardian had risen when his name was called, or nodded if he was already standing. Some—most, in fact—of the audience applauded. There were exceptions, notably several men in trim tan pseudouniforms who stood in a group near the far wall, beneath a really bad painting of a bullfight scene. Morgenstern had warned the Guardians there were going to be people here they wouldn't be happy to see, and McKay was willing to guess that these were some of them.

"Thanks, Doctor," he said with more than his customary gruffness. Being put on the spot like this had him off-balance, though he should have expected it. "You gotta understand right off, nobody's bulletproof, not even us—but neither are the Effsees. The only reason we have a chance of pushing them out of California now is the troubles in Europe you've probably heard of. But we *do* have a chance, and if you all do your parts we might just kick some ass." He should have stopped there, but he really hadn't thought out what he was saying.

"One more thing. I know you're used to doing your own things. Well, that's just fine. But this army ain't a democracy. We got to keep our act together. If you cross us up, we'll have to hurt you. That's, uh, that's all I got to say."

Everybody stared at him in resounding silence, bro-

ken only when Sam Sloan brought his forehead down
on his table with a thump. Morgenstern was looking as
if somebody'd slipped a rotten onion in his robes.
McKay's ears burned. *So I stepped on my dick again.
Well, if Morgenstern wanted a public speaker, he
should have gotten fucking David Letterman,* he
thought.

"Lieutenant McKay is very concerned that everyone
understand the gravity of the situation," Morgenstern
said. "He's a man who believes in direct speech as well
as direct action."

Sloan coughed loudly. McKay turned away toward
the bar. He should have primed Sam to say a few words;
he was good at that sort of thing. And now Morgenstern
was introducing Sloan, who was supposed to outline the
plan the Guardians had worked out with the doctor.

"Got any Coors?" McKay asked the chipmunk.

The bartender's eyes sidled left and right. He nodded.
"But it'll cost you."

McKay nodded. He looked off toward the bandstand,
where Sam was doing his amiable hayseed shtick. He
looked back at the chipmunk.

"Listen, Jack, this bar is full of escaped doorknobs
who are armed to the teeth. One of 'em's even wearing a
sword, for Chrissake."

The bartender's eyes slipped from McKay's again,
skipped over the crowd. They were round when they
looked back at the ex-marine.

"Now, it would take only a few words to make 'em
all crazy. Then they'd take this joint apart. As it is I
think maybe we can keep them under control, but I ain't
promising nothing."

He crossed his thick forearms on the bar and hung his
face in the bartender's. "Now, let's try it again. You got
a Coors?"

"On the house, sir."

He took the beer and sat at a table occupied only by Bonnie Sanchez, who had a Swiss Army knife as thick as an L.A. phone book. She was flipping through the blades and attachments as if hoping to turn up one nobody'd ever spotted before. She grinned at him as he sat down.

"You know any of these people?"

"Oh, sure. We get all the gossip in the castle. Can I see that?" She was reaching for his chest. Engrossed in his beer—chilled, by Christ!—he didn't react until he felt a tug on his shirt and behind his ear, and realized she was trying to fish his communicator out of its pocket.

"Wait a minute," he said, clapping a hand over the pocket-calculator–sized radio. "Gimme that back."

She pouted. "I just wanted to look at it."

"It's top-secret."

She looked at him.

He thought about it a moment, then took out the microphone, unplugged the throat mike and earphone jacks, and handed it over.

"So who're those detached assholes over by the wall?" he asked, jerking his head toward the tan para-military types.

She had the communicator's case open. McKay felt a twinge. "People's Republic of the Bear," she said. "Leader's Von Lewis—guy with the blond mustache. Call him the Red Baron."

McKay almost swallowed his beer. The closest he'd ever been to emissaries of the People's Republic of the Bear had been when he and the other Guardians shot a bunch of them loose from Balin's Forge just north of L.A. last year. They'd been some of van Damm's staunchest supporters until they finally got a bellyful of him and joined the revolt that forced him to flee his headquarters in the old Hearst Castle.

"Then there's Neil Mixson." She nodded at a lean bearded man in khaki shorts and a Minnesota Twins baseball cap. "He's a real asshole. Sons of Hayduke; eco-guerrilla types. Tried to sabotage us a couple of times, before the Effsees turned up. Then there's some guy calling himself Sir Reynard Fitz-Morris from the Duchy of New Carolina." That was the man with the sword. "And there's those sea gypsy women—I think they're kinda creepy—and Idaho and Lancelot from the Forge, but I guess you know them. And the short woman with the mustache is Martha Gambatelli, she's from the San Joaquin Feminist Commune, but I don't think she's you know, funny. And there's Frank Watts from Tulare, represents small farmers, and my Uncle Luis from Dos Palos, and—"

"What about the curly-haired guy with the mouth?"

"Phil Duvall. Bay-Area type. Effsees shot his brother. He got a big guerrilla band together after that, what the Effsees call bandits. Nothing political, not like the Bear Republic people. They all just hate Effsees real hard. They say he's pretty wild, though."

"Great." He drained the can. He noticed that Morgenstern and Sloan were looking at him fixedly, realized he'd just heard his name mentioned.

"Uh, gotta run—time to go save the world." He stood up, started off, pulled up short, and turned back to collect his communicator. "Thank you."

"You're welcome." She held up a piece of molded plastic. "Say, don't you want the back of it?"

It was ten o'clock by the fat and fancy watch strapped to McKay's wrist, and gosh, it hardly seemed like seven hours. It seemed more like at least a week.

But things had been accomplished. With a minimum of overt intimidation and threats—which even McKay dimly acknowledged weren't the swiftest forms of personnel management—the disparate elements of Morgenstern's expanded network had agreed to the plan of scattered, seemingly random attacks on Effsee strength in the North. Only two groups had stomped out (after having it impressed on them that the Guardians were well armed and knew where they lived, in case they were planning any lapses of discretion within earshot of the occupying forces) and there had been no more than three fistfights—only one of which had involved McKay at the outset. He hadn't started that one, either, and when he finished it with one jolt to the bulbous red face of the beefy scavenger from San Jose most of the onlookers applauded.

Now he was holding down the bar top, eating fresh fried pork skins from a plastic mixing bowl and talking with Bonnie, who was busy rebuilding a drink mixer with a burnt-out motor. She wasn't suitable mattress fodder, even by his somewhat lax standards, but for some reason he found her easy to hang out with. Just like one of the guys, almost.

He caught Tom Rogers's eye across the room, gestured with his bottle—Miller, this time; the chipmunk had insisted he was out of Coors, and McKay hadn't felt like browbeating him anymore.

"How's it going?" he asked the compact ex–Green Beret when he walked up.

Rogers nodded politely to Bonnie, helped himself to a handful of crackly pork skins. "All right, I think."

"Is this whole scheme gonna work?"

Rogers shrugged. "Can't tell in advance. We got a few vets and a lot of eager amateurs. They're still indiges, which means they ain't gonna be too reliable."

"Indiges?" Bonnie asked.

"Indigenous forces." Tom offered her the bowl.

"Euu. No thanks. They're fried; too much choles-
terol."

"I figured you kids would like fried stuff," McKay
remarked.

"Roger—he's our satellite-uplink expert—turned us
on to healthy foods."

"Son of a bitch," McKay remarked. "So, Tom, can
they do the job?"

Rogers shrugged. "Funny thing about Americans.
They're the most spoiled people in history, they're self-
indulgent, they lose interest real quick, they can't take
hardship. Mostly. But get 'em good and pissed-off,
there's nothing they won't do, nothing they won't put
up with. Bartender?"

The chipmunk came up with a Dr. Pepper chilled by
an alcohol-fired compressor, for which Tom gave him a
couple of pre-1965 dimes, much valued as post-holocaust currency because of their high silver content and
convenient size. If he knew McKay'd been extorting
beers from the man he'd tear him a new asshole; he was
a big believer in keeping right with the populace, like
most Green Beanies.

"I reckon the Effsees have about got these folks
pissed off enough," he said. "Beg pardon, ma'am."

Bonnie made an easy negatory gesture. Then she bit
her lip and shrank back. McKay frowned, then looked
the way she was looking, back over his shoulder.

Donna and Lori were standing there. "McKay," Lori
said, gesturing with a hand that held a bottle of Hein-
eken and a slim black cigar clipped between first and
second fingers.

"How they hangin', Lori?" McKay said.

"What, my ovaries? Fine, just fine." She barked a

laugh and gouged McKay in the ribs. Bonnie bolted.

Lori was a short woman with a bulldog build and an Oliver Hardy haircut. McKay nodded past her at her lover Donna, a tall, gangly woman with short brown hair, a deepwater tan, and a perpetually apologetic expression. Under most circumstances McKay had no use for lezzies, but these two had long ago established themselves in his eyes as Good Troop, which transcended all other classifications. By taking them as offbeat men he found them easy to get along with, though Lori occasionally reminded him of a drill instructor he had in boot camp.

"Ms. Kennedy, Ms. Lombardi," Tom said politely.

"Tommy." Lori nodded, turned back to McKay. "We got a problem, Guardian."

"What, you want out already?"

"No way. We want the Effsees gone as much as anybody. Maybe even more—evening, Commodore."

The last was to the newly arrived Sloan. "Howdy, Lori, Donna. What seems to be the matter? I thought you didn't concern yourselves much with landlubber affairs."

"Well . . . we don't much like to, but we seem to be tied up in them anyway. The kicker is that your damned landlubber difficulties have started spilling out into the sea like your garbage used to."

"How do you mean?" McKay asked.

"Pirates," Donna said in her soft high voice. "They're killing us."

"Well, now, I thought we'd given you some ideas how to cope with them," Sloan said. He'd taught an ad hoc antipiracy course during the Guardians' earlier stay in California, which had earned him the nickname "Commodore" from the sea gypsies.

"Yeah, you did, so you can quit fishing for compliments," Lori said around her cigar. "But they're coming back—with help from the fucking FSE.

"Military government's got a hair up its butt about stamping on the black market. They're especially concerned with us seafolk—'smugglers,' I think is the word they use. So they deputized a bunch of the pirates, been refueling and refitting them down south, supplying them with weapons."

"How well organized are these pirates?" Tom asked.

"Not very well," Donna offered. "But then they don't have to be. Even using what Commander Sloan taught us, we don't have the, the firepower to stand up to them."

"So you're saying these pirate assholes are working with the Effsees?" McKay said, rubbing his jaw.

"Yeah. Why? Don't you believe me?" Lori jutted her own jaw pugnaciously.

"Oh, we believe you, Ms. Kennedy," Tom said. "They're using the pirates the way they use the road gypsies other places."

"Which means these pirates are legitimate targets for our campaign to get the Effsees lined out and headed in the right direction," Sloan finished. "I think we'll be able to lend you ladies a hand."

Lori scowled. "Who're you calling a lady?"

"I'm not sure how soon we can do anything, though," Tom said. "We got a lot on our plate."

"Please hurry," Donna said. "They're killing us . . . lots of us."

"Say, have you guys seen Idaho and Lancelot?" Casey asked, coming up with a rare worried expression on his face. "I can't find them anywhere. Hi, Lori, Donna."

McKay looked around the barroom. Despite the dragon poster a haze of cigarette smoke hung like a rock stratum at head height. The meeting had broken up into little knots clustered at the tables. "Can't see 'em. Maybe they had to get back to the Forge in a hurry."

"Lieutenant McKay."

"Hey, I'm a popular kind of guy." He turned toward the voice and felt the muscles of his face freeze.

"Red Baron" Lewis stood there, an athletic, squared-away-looking man in tan, with a slightly modified California flag patch sewn on the short right sleeve of his shirt. The real state flag sported a red star as it was; this version had a tiny hammer and sickle in red to the right and below it, and the legend People's Republic under the bear. He wore an H&K P-7 in a matching flapped cordura holster.

McKay looked him up and down and said nothing. The PRB boys had always gone in for snappy dressing. The Che Guevara look was apparently passé—understandable, given Che's success record, which wasn't great. He looked fit and from the lines in his handsome face he was probably older than he looked, maybe mid-thirties, a year or two older than McKay.

"You don't trust me, Lieutenant," Lewis said.

"Just to keep the air clear between us allies," McKay said, "no. I don't. You're a no-good commie sonofa-bitch."

The Red Baron accepted a glass of white wine from the chipmunk. "And you're a running-dog lackey of a defunct capitalist empire." He raised the glass in salute, drank. "Now we have the amenities out of the way. We have been enemies in the past, McKay, and we'll probably be enemies again in the future, unless of course you realize the futility of resisting the historic necessity of socialism's triumph."

"Fat chance."

"However, at present our interests coincide. The Federated States of Europe imposes an unbearable burden on the working classes of the former state of California. They are, to speak frankly, a greater threat than you.''

"Thanks a whole hell of a lot."

Lewis grinned. "Don't tell me you're not thinking the same thing." After a moment McKay grinned back. "All right. I just want you to understand: the forces of the People's Republic are cooperating wholeheartedly in all actions against our mutual enemy, even as we agreed this evening. We will keep our faith.''

McKay turned away. " 'The check is in the mail.' 'The choppers are on their way.' Yeah, I've heard lines like that before."

The Red Baron's face changed to match his name. "Think what you want to, McKay. But when this is over, see if you will be able to look me in the eye and say we went back on our word."

"I'll do that," McKay said sourly. "*Trust* me."

CHAPTER
NINE ────────────────

Susan Spinelli woke from a dark turbulent dream to the feel of a man's hand over her mouth.

The room was black. Moonlight filtered through cloud and pines shone through the double-paned window to silver the plastic housing of the personal computer on the desk next to her cot. *It's Buddy!* she thought in sudden terror, and repented the impulse that led her to make her bed alone in her office instead of sleeping in the dorms with the others.

Belatedly she thought to fight back, trying to jack-knife her body, thrashing furiously with fists and feet. She managed to upset the cot and her rump hit the hardwood floor with a thump.

"Jesus Christ," a voice hissed in her ear. "Will you calm down? It's me. Sam."

She fought a moment more before abruptly running out of steam. Her mind told her it was improbable, but her nose registered the familiarity of the smell of the hard male body pressed to hers. She quit struggling.

Tentatively the intruder relaxed his grip. Susan turned to look at him in the moonlight backscatter. She recoiled; what she confronted was alien, inhuman. Then white teeth grinned at her, she saw the crescent sparkle of starlight on eyeballs, and the image rearranged itself into something sensible. The face was smeared with a base of black, with smudges of gray and green and brown across it to break up the distinctive contours of human features, but it indisputably belonged to Commander Samuel Sloan, formerly of the U.S. Navy.

"I thought you slept naked," he said.

"I used to." *As you well know, Sam Sloan.* "But I've taken to wearing this dowdy *Grapes of Wrath* nightgown so certain people won't get . . . ideas."

Then she threw herself against him and hugged him with startling strength. She couldn't quite keep her sob inside.

"So you have returned to New Eden," Dr. Georges Mahalaby said, blinking sleepily and trying to get his specs settled in on his nose, the shape of which resembled something he might have grown in his high-powered garden. "We knew you would, of course. Still, I do not know if it is best; it is very dangerous for you."

The Lebanese-born agronomist was making a good-faith effort to keep his voice down. What emerged from his beer-keg chest was a basso rumble that rattled the windows of his darkened office. Wincing, McKay glanced at the fluorescent glow, which cut a line through darkness at the bottom of the door. The lights burned all night long in the corridor outside, by orders of the expeditionary force. No telltale shadows of boots at the door broke the line, but McKay was wary. He and Sam had spotted several uniformed FSE regulars patrolling the compound when they had infiltrated New Eden from the wooded hip of Maldita Peak.

"This is just a friendly visit, Doc," McKay explained in the sub-conversational tone of voice they'd taught him was less conspicuous than a whisper back in his SOG-SWAC days. Like Sloan his face was painted like a New York subway car, and he had a stubby little silenced MP-5 in his hands in case the Effsees got frisky. "Wanted to say hi, see the sights, find out how things looked for when we came back on business."

"What my esteemed leader means to say," Sloan said, "is that we're here on reconnaissance. We're hoping we can liberate the commune some day . . . soon."

Sitting squeezed in next to him on the floor between Mahalaby's paper-piled desk and a filing cabinet, with her knees up and her thin flannel nightgown pulled tightly around her, Susan inhaled sharply, gave his hand an eager squeeze.

"I understood that, yes," Mahalaby said. "But I am afraid it will do no good. New Eden is important to the Federated States of Europe, you see, just as it is important to America. If you free us, all that will happen is they will send more men and more guns to take it back. And they . . . they are such that if they cannot have the fruits of our valley they will make sure no one else does, in such a twisted way have they grown."

He sat there on a swivel chair with his hairy legs protruding from his boxer shorts, his gray-shot black hair flowing around his massive shoulders, looking like an agitated shaggy Buddha, turning a cutting from some kind of tree over and over in his great hands.

"Listen, Doc, we have reason to believe that real soon now the Effsees might not be in a position to come back if we kick them out." McKay was moving around the cramped office, picking up this or that, putting it back down. He knew he was fidgeting, but he couldn't help it. Snooping and pooping in here like this had worked him up, had put him in a fit of weird excitement like some kind of kid recruit. It was a hell of a way for a past master of infiltration to be acting. *I gotta quit playing politician so fucking much and get back to more real, live soldiering,* he thought.

Mahalaby raised his head, his eyebrows sweeping upward like fern fronds in a wind.

"I can't say more'n that right now," McKay told him. "But I can tell you that we won't make a move unless we're pretty sure the Effsees can't make a comeback."

"*Doctor,*" Susan breathed. Her eyes were fixed on Mahalaby, and Sam felt a twinge of jealousy at the adoration he saw in them.

Mahalaby nodded. "What is it you wish to know, gentlemen?"

"What's the setup? How many men they got here, how're they armed, all like that."

At first, FSE strength in the commune didn't seem too impressive: roughly a squad, about twenty men armed mostly with rifles, plus at least one machine gun and several weapons the two Guardians judged were grenade launchers. There were also fat tubes made of what looked like fiberglass that could only be antitank rocket launchers. Since the death of the facility's security chief, Ari Lavotsky, there'd been nobody with any military experience hereabouts, but both the doctor and Spinelli were excellent observers, and McKay quickly learned enough to convince him that the Guardians themselves could deal with the FSE troopies.

But they weren't the whole story. "You know of course," the doctor said, "that General Edwards is now officially in charge of our facility."

"Mother*fucker,*" McKay said with simple conviction. "I knew we should have shortened that gimped cocksucker by a head."

Sam looked grim behind his warpaint. That was the

kind of extreme talk he usually despaired of in his commander, but at the moment he happened to agree one
hundred percent. The Guardians had been forced to
deal briskly with New Eden's neighbors before. Active
before the war in the ultrarightist paramilitary organiza-
tion known as the California Free Militia, former Air
Force General Manton Edwards was the none-too-
benevolent dictator of Edwards's Valley across the ridge
from New Eden. He'd had designs on the laboratory-
cum-commune since before the war. During the great
van Damm H-bomb crisis he—or at least a trusted
lieutenant—had made a takeover play. The Guardians
blocked it; Edwards blamed everything on the overzeal-
ousness of the henchman, who'd been used up in the
process; and that, since the Guardians had more pressing business, had been that.

"And this somebody you wanted to discourage?"
Sloan said to Susan.

"Buddy Donner." The Donner clan shared power
with the general in Edwards's Valley, lording it over a
couple of hundred "civilians" who enjoyed serf status.

"That fat little fuck?" McKay said. He'd picked up a
little orange flowerpot with a tiny pale tentacle of seed-
ling poking up out of it, was holding it in front of his
nose as if he could actually tell asparagus from opium
poppies. "What about big brother Randy? He was the
real stud, the way I remember it."

Susan moistened thin pale lips. "He, ah, he has interests of his own." Her eyes flicked to Dr. Mahalaby.

He lowered his huge head till his beard trailed on his
paunch. "Anna," he said in a hollow whisper. "Anna
Yoshimitsu. He . . . took her."

The flowerpot crumbled as McKay's fist convulsed
shut. Black dirt, orange clay shards, and drops of blood
fell onto the wooden floor. McKay had had a fling with
Anna Yoshimitsu during their earlier stay in New Eden.

It was just that, a good time for both, nothing like what seemed to have sprung up between Sloan and Susan Spinelli. But McKay felt proprietary about any woman he'd slept with.

"What the fuck?" he demanded. "Why'd you let him do that? Didn't anybody *do* something?"

A tear rolled down Mahalaby's pomegranate cheek.

"What could we do?" hissed Susan Spinelli, half in anger, half in apology. "We're not fighters here. He had some of his goons with him, and the Federated States soldiers didn't interfere—he's on *their* side. How could we have stopped him?"

McKay knew the answer: they couldn't. Had any of the gentle, spacy scientists tried, the Effsees would have blown them away.

Voices from the corridor froze them momentarily in place. Then Sam was crouched behind the desk with his submachine gun at the ready, Susan curled out of sight beside him, while McKay flattened himself against a filing cabinet back of the door and stood there with the big leaves of the potted plant on top of the cabinet falling all over his face, waiting. Mahalaby simply sat amid the plants and papers on his desk, huge and fatalistic. If the Effsees found the Guardians here and now, they'd almost certainly get away clean. But what would happen to the occupants of New Eden after that didn't bear thinking about.

The voices passed on down the corridor. Sam turned and kissed Susan quickly. "We've got to go."

"But we'll be back," Billy McKay said.

Camp Ed Meese was a collection of olive drab tents and liberated house trailers twenty dusty klicks north of Tulare, arranged in orderly ranks around a parade ground and a flagpole with the Stars and Stripes hanging from it in the breezeless day—and slumped over it, all but obscuring it in its folds, the blue map of Europe encircled in a field of white of the Federated States of Europe. It wasn't much of a place, maybe half a klick square, but the 32nd Brigade (Mixed) of the FSE expeditionary force, whose area of operations included the central San Joaquin Valley, called it home. They called it lots of other things, too, in several different languages.

The sun was barely up and the day was already much too hot for almost October when a deuce-and-a-half done up in mottled desert camouflage came dragging into camp, riding low on its suspension. At the gate the driver stopped and poked computer-printout orders at the sentry. As it happened the sentry was Dutch, and neither spoke nor read English, but he did recognize the form and the authentication sequences and destination code for Camp Ed.

He gave the occupants the once-over, just to be doing something. Both had on U.S. Army OD fatigues with FSE shoulder patches. The driver was a compact man who raised his cap and mopped at the sweat crossing his hairline's line of retreat with an OD handkerchief. The passenger was a lanky dude kind of spilled up against the far door jawing on a chunk of gum, with longish blond hair falling out from beneath his forage cap and his eyes hidden by regulation Third World dictator mirror shades. He grinned at the sentry, punctuated it by blowing a pink bubble. He held out a dogeared pack of gum.

The sentry hesitated. Bubble gum was on the list of Non-Necessity Items proscribed by the government in Sacramento (which had recently pulled up stakes and moved south in something of a hurry). A civilian could be detained for suspicion of black-market activities or unlicensed scavenging just for possessing it, and even soldiers weren't supposed to have it. Of course they all took it when they could get it, like all the other good things they weren't supposed to have. The sentry accepted a stick, smiled, thanked them politely in Dutch, and waved them through.

Engine laboring, the truck cruised in past a couple of parked M-60 tanks, past a dozen or so Cadillac Gage V-150 armored cars with long snouted 20-mm cannon in their turrets—smaller ancestors of the ten-ton V-450 the infamous Guardians, rumored to have returned to the state, rode around in—and assorted trucks, jeeps, and hummers.

Troops were drilling on the grounds when the deuce-and-a-half groaned to a stop in front of the admin trailers. The brigade's West German commander was a notorious hardass, who believed idle troops were, well, idle. He believed in keeping 'em busy, no matter how uselessly.

A clerk-lieutenant in French uniform came bouncing down the steps of the trailer. "No parking," he yelled at the two men climbing down from the cab. "No park here at all."

The tall one waved a clipboard with a sheaf of pastel forms stuck to it like butterflies pinned to a board. "Captain Potsnerd, man. We need his signature."

"*Qu'est-ce que vous avez dit?*"

"Potsnerd, man, Potsnerd. Captain."

The clerk-lieutenant shook his head. He'd never heard of any such man, but that barely surprised him; these thick-tongued barbarians could scarcely speak their own language. He returned to his earlier demand that they remove the truck *tout de suite.* Instead they turned and walked away, carrying jackets in their hands. For a moment he stared after them as they ambled off toward the motor pool, then threw up his hands and went back to his desk.

The two American squaddies went smoking and joking through the transport park until they were back out of sight of the mechanics overhauling various vehicles. Then the tall one in the shades got into a cute little German open-top Volkswagen jeep, and began to fiddle with it while the shorter, stockier one leaned on the hood smoking, his jacket folded over his right arm.

A mechanic walked around the fender of a canvas-back truck wiping his hands on a piece of waste. "Hey," he said, "why are you messing with that? That's Captain Broussard's—"

He didn't get any further. The square-built man standing by the jeep let his jacket slip from his arm. Beneath it he held an old-fashioned Government Model Colt .45 with a silencer screwed onto the end of it. While the mechanic stood and goggled the man shot him twice through the heart. The only noise was a double metallic thud, like somebody pounding a recalcitrant piece of equipment, and the much softer sound of a lifeless body hitting the hard-packed earth.

The rhythm of sounds around, the mechanical noises and voices shouting conversation and the whistles and shouts out on the parade ground, never changed. After a moment the stocky man stepped forward, took the hapless mechanic by the collar of his coveralls, dragged him between two deuce-and-a-halfs, and rolled him beneath one.

The *Kübelwagen*'s engine hiccuped into life. "Got it, Tom," the lanky soldier said. The man walked back, picked up his jacket, and climbed in. They drove off.

They had a fresh set of orders for the sentry at the gate. The Dutch kid thought it was a bit strange for the pair to arrive by truck and leave so quickly in a jeep, but orders were orders, and this wasn't his damn country anyway. The VW drove off, wheels raising a bit of dust from the road that led between derelict beanfields to paved highway.

• • •

Ten minutes later Colonel Preiss was standing in front
of his headquarters trailer demanding to know why
there was a truck parked there. His little French clerk-
lieutenant stood by making shrill excuses about undis-
ciplined Americans until he'd had enough, which didn't
take real long.

He turned to his adjutant. "Have somebody move the
damned thing. And shut *him* up."

"*Jawohl, Herr Oberst.*"

After the moment or two it took to root up somebody
of rank lowly enough to permit him to move a truck, an
eighteen-year-old squaddie from Cologne clambered
into the cab and turned the key. The engine turned over,
caught, and the generator sent a pulse to half a dozen
electrical detonators fixed to plastic-explosive squibs
embedded in a thousand kilograms of diesel-oil-impreg-
nated chemical fertilizer. Another thousand kilos of
metal scrap (assorted) rode the blast wave outward and
obliterated the truck, the squaddie from Cologne,
Colonel Preiss, his adjutant, the little French lieutenant,
the admin trailers, and a hundred or so luckless con-
scripts from the Rhine Valley.

Five klicks away Casey Wilson heard the blast and
glanced back to see a black column of smoke pluming
up into the sky. "I guess somebody tried to move the
truck." He shuddered.

Riding beside him, Tom Rogers shrugged. A timer
would have set the charge off in a few more minutes
anyway. He didn't look back.

CHAPTER
TEN

Like a giant, gleaming metal dachshund the tanker crawled around a bend in Highway 1 not far from San Simeon. In front of it rolled a green V-150 with FSE insignia painted on its bow, its 20-mm automatic cannon barrel jutting like an insect's proboscis. Behind the tanker came a pair of deuce-and-a-halfs carrying a couple of squads of troops. A hummer mounting a Dover .50-caliber had already passed around a curve and out of sight of the bluff overlooking the road. The Effsees weren't taking any chances with this precious fuel, looted from the North and now following the military government south.

Beyond the road the rocky yellow land tumbled steeply to the sea. Inland it pitched upward even more abruptly, forming a yellow forehead crested with a brush-cut of scrub. Half a dozen men and women were lying in the scrub watching with binoculars shaded so

their lenses wouldn't reflect the sun and give them away
to the convoy below.

Von Lewis—the People's Republic of the Bear officer
known to all as the Red Baron—found the situation
gently ironic. Both his comrades and the Sons—and
Daughter—of Hayduke hunkered in the bush here with
them had visited the none-too-distant Hearst Castle as
allies before, when it was headquarters to Geoff van
Damm's California Liberation Front, of which both
their groups were members. The Guardians and Morgenstern's network had been their enemies then.

Now, here they were, allies again, only this time fighting on the Guardians' side. The Red Baron found the
historical process inscrutable sometimes. At times it actually seemed to display a sense of humor.

He adjusted the focus of the binoculars as the shiny
tanker rolled closer. "If you're going to shoot that
thing," he said sidelong, "you'd better do it quickly."

"I just wanted to savor the moment," Neil Mixson
said. He reared up in his bush and brought the long,
skinny RPG-7 launcher to his shoulder. His male and
female companion knelt close to him in almost reveren-
tial attitudes.

Glancing sideways uneasily—he wasn't too sure how
far to trust a hater of technology with a technological
device, even one as simple as an antitank rocket—the
Red Baron wondered if one of them wasn't going to
genuflect right into the backblast. He halfway hoped so.
He hadn't much liked the monkeywrenchers when they
were in CLF together, either.

Mixson squinted through the optical sight, a taut,
peculiar grin on his face. To his alarm Lewis saw the
man's hands were shaking. He dropped the binoculars
and picked up the AKM assault rifle lying by his side.

"Fucking land rapers," Mixson was muttering to

himself like some kind of litany. "Exploiters. Machine-worshiping bastards."

"For Christ's sake, calm down," Lewis said. "I want it as badly as you do." *Badly enough to kill you and fire the rocket myself if you can't get control of yourself.*

"He's right, Neil," said the dark-haired man in jeans and split-soled sharkskin cowboy boots. He patted his friend reassuringly on the shoulder.

"What are you waiting for," the blond woman hissed. "Shoot! I want to see the bastards burn."

Mixson's finger convulsed on the trigger. The rocket hissed away from the tube, the main motor caught, and the spindle-shaped projectile buzzed down to hit the swollen silver tank squarely as the truck went broadside to them not a hundred meters away. Lewis buried his face in his arms as the shaped-charge warhead went off with a crack.

There was a *whoosh*, which sounded large rather than loud. Heat washed over Lewis like a tsunami.

Cautiously he peered over his arm. Through a tangle of ginger-colored hairs he saw the tanker had veered into the shoulder of the bluff and lay in the middle of an expanding oval of fire. The first truck following had already been swallowed up, and the bright sparks moving around the fire-wrapped shadow shape were burning men. The firestorm rolled back to encompass the cab of the next truck in line. The driver cranked the wheel in blind panic—the deuce-and-a-half rolled off the road, jolting out of control down the slope toward the surf, cab aflame, soldiers bouncing helplessly out the back.

Mixson and his companions were jumping up and down, whooping and cheering. The Red Baron exchanged disbelieving glances with Comrade Jesse and Comrade Fred and the three of them turned and went wading down the back side of the forehead in miniature landslides of rocks and dirt.

The burning gasoline had not reached the V-150, and it was royally pissed off. The three Haydukians were still doing their victory dance in plain view of the road and the entire Pacific Ocean when its twenty mike-mike cut loose in a snarling burst. A shell caught the blond woman below the left breast as she was jumping up with her tangled hair flying all around and exploded.

The three PRB men were already at the base of the bluff where the two pickups were parked, and were now looking back. "Assholes," Comrade Jesse said.

Mixson and his friend came lurching down the hill with their beards streaming tears, supporting the woman between them. "Carrying" would be a better word; the round had blown her rib cage open, and her innards were spewing out. Comrade Fred turned aside and threw up on the Chevy's right rear tire.

"Leave her," the Red Baron said.

The two had fought the Toyota's door open and were trying to cram the lifeless body inside. It kept folding in inconvenient ways, and tangles of flash-cooked guts kept getting underfoot. Lewis's breakfast had been modest, but he could feel it deciding he was going to see it again real soon.

"She's our sister," the black-haired man said, flopping an arm into the cab. "We gotta help her."

A real Mount St. Helens cloud of black smoke was shouldering up toward the stratosphere from the far side of the bluff. The 20-mm was still working the crestline as if planning to saw right down through it after them. The area would definitely not be healthy for long.

"She's dead," Lewis said. "Dump her and let's go."

"But she's too beautiful to die."

"Right." The three climbed into the Chevy and drove off.

"*Bourgeois* assholes," Comrade Jesse observed from behind the wheel.

Comrade Fred was hanging his head out the window, rubbing his face with sand to get the puke off it. "Somehow I don't think they're politically mature enough for this kind of thing, Comrade Von."

Riding in the middle, the Red Baron glanced into the rearview mirror. Mixson and his friend were still trying to convince the dead woman to get into the beige Toyota. As he watched an arm came off in the black-bearded man's hand, who then sat down, crossed his arms over his knees, and buried his head in them, still holding the lolling arm like a talisman.

"Somehow I think you're right."

Sam Sloan walked hunched over, willing himself to weightlessness. No matter how hard he tried he couldn't keep the crepe soles of his boots from making scrunching sounds on the pebbles under the windows of the erstwhile motel. When they did it rang in his ears as loud as glass breaking.

He froze at a particularly awful crunch. The moon was down, but if anybody looked out he was going to see a large, darkish lump of former naval officer out here on all this damned light-colored gravel. He huddled the little blocks of Composition C-4 and the festoons of fuse that held them together against his chest and waited, not even daring to breathe.

"For God's sake, now what's the hang-up?" McKay's voice demanded in his ear. He jumped, almost lost his balance.

"Nothing," Sloan whispered urgently, too rattled to recall McKay could hear him whether any sound left his mouth or not.

"Well, for Christ's sake get a move on. These

damned indiges are liable to start busting caps on their own if you take much longer."

"Jesus."

One thing being a Guardian had done to Sam was to forever diminish his faith in the innate common sense of humanity. He used to regard the mistrust in which McKay and Rogers held indiges as demeaning and elitist. Now the only reason he had consented to plant the string of small explosive charges along the front wall of this wing of the one-story motel was that he knew McKay had hold of the detonator, and would do anything to keep hold of it, up to and including killing anybody who tried to lay hands on it. Sam was a brave man, but this little jaunt was risky enough without taking the chance some local hero's buck fever, fear, or fanaticism would atomize him at any random moment.

The last was the most likely possibility. This particular mission was very popular among the indigenous elements. Because here they weren't striking so much at Effsee troops as at a regional barracks of the hated popular forces—a police force recruited from local law-enforcement officers leavened with stragglers and deserters from the military and assorted civilian lowlifes of the variety who aspire to have official sanction to talk mean, bust heads, and shoot anyone who looks at them with both eyes simultaneously. The expeditionary forces often acted like conquerors, but conquerors throughout history had acted benevolently at times, and unless they had faced stiff resistance (which the FSE mostly had not) usually treated the locals with indifference.

The popular forces had axes to grind. They wanted to swagger in front of the home folks, to make their old enemies eat turd. They tended to act like Mongols on angel dust. Rape, robbery, murder, and torture—frequently the only thing that tempered the PF taste for such sports was the boredom of sheer satiety. Finding volunteers for this mission had been no problem —finding ones who didn't have such overwhelming personal grudges with the PFs that they'd be uncontrollable had been next to impossible.

Following guidelines Tom had laid down before he had headed south with Casey to spread the word and scope out L.A., McKay had weeded out the obvious unreliables such as those who'd had loved ones raped or killed by the PFs, and former law-enforcement agents, whose hatred for their turncoat former comrades ran to the pathological. That hadn't left many. Nor was he thrilled that the selection process gave him the firebrand Phil Duvall as second in command, but Duvall was one of the very few people in California who hated the FSE regulars more than their popular force auxiliaries.

Sam was very conscious of all this, which didn't make it any easier to concentrate on silently emplacing the charges. He was feeling more than a little internal upset with this whole thing as it was. It smacked to him of plain murder. Whatever these PFs were, whatever they had done—

A flicker in his peripheral vision snapped his eyes up and right to the picture window just above his head. His body turned to stone. A woman stood there, naked, pale as an apparition in the starlight, gazing out at the scrub where McKay and the guerrillas lurked and brushing absently at dark hair that spilled down over her shoulders. Her breasts were full, the nipples dark as ink.

Sloan's pulsebeat sounded a drumroll in his ears. The thought that he held in his hands a small block that would shortly tear that lovely body to bloody shreds nauseated him. For a moment it was all he could do not to puke.

The sudden fear of discovery drove the sickness

from him. Had it not been for the glass he could have stretched out his right hand and brushed the dark wedge of her pubic hair. All she had to do was glance down —how could she not see him? He was out there in the open, he was caught . . .

She turned and swayed back into the recesses of the room. Sloan let out a shaky breath. He had damned near pissed his pants.

"Whoo," McKay whistled in his ear. "She was a looker. Pity to mess up a piece like that."

"McKay, you insensitive bastard!" Sloan hissed. "How can you talk about a human being like that?"

"You're just uptight because it's a woman, and a foxy one at that," McKay taunted. "Ain't that a bit sexist, Mr. Women's Liberation?"

The skin tightened at Sam's temples. He was furious with McKay, the more so because he was absolutely right. "I can't do it," he subvocalized.

"This is war, Navy boy. Now get your ass in gear—or do you wanna stay down there doing your imitation of a shrub and playing Peeping Tom?"

Sloan grimaced. His fingers worked quickly at the block of Composition C-4. He lacked Tom Rogers's artistry with explosives, but Guardians training had made a demolitions expert of him. He shorted the wire tied to the electronic fuse stuck into the plastic block, so that the current would travel down the line without setting this charge off. Then he emplaced the remaining charges and went pelting back to join the others.

"This . . . this is terrorism, pure and simple," he puffed as he threw himself down next to McKay.

Lying on his belly on the caliche with an unlit stub of cigar in his mouth and the detonator in his hands, McKay cocked an eyebrow at him. "No shit."

"You mean you admit it?" Sam asked in stunned

disbelief. "You mean we're no different from the PLO or Baader-Meinhof?"

"Well, we ain't blowing up a shopping mall full of kids and old ladies. These here're legitimate enemies. Other than that—hell, no, why should we be different? You got a small group goin' up against a much stronger force, you got to resort to psychological warfare. Which is fancy talk for terrorism."

"But that woman—" Sloan said, gesturing toward the darkened motel.

Around them the partisans were stirring and grumbling. "The charges," Duvall was whispering fiercely, hunched over behind a bush a few meters away. "What are you waiting for? Set off the charges!"

"A collaborator," McKay said, giving Duvall an ugly look.

"But she's unarmed! There must be others—"

"The purpose of terror is to terrorize," McKay said. "Lenin said that." He twisted the detonator.

With a rippling crack the charges exploded. Glass splinters and chunks of cinder block scythed into the PFs asleep or otherwise occupied on their beds, riding the shock wave. Fire leapt. People screamed.

The partisans opened fire with weapons ranging from deer rifles to fully automatic AKMs. Figures staggering through smoke, weeping and coughing and beating at flames on their clothes, fell as the barrage ripped into them. Duvall laughed like a madman, and he wasn't the only one.

McKay had the M-60's bipod down, the black butt snugged against his shoulder, and was walking fire back and forth across the front of the building. He wasn't aiming; as far as he was concerned this raid had more to do with putting the righteous fear up these pukes than killing a lot of them, however much they might deserve it. On the other hand, when his copper-jacketed slugs sent a figure spinning into the flames scampering up the curtains and feeding greedily on torn mattresses he wasn't devastated, either.

Sloan lay immobile by his side. His face was fixed, deep lines dug in at the corners of his mouth and eyes, and dead pale—a canvas painted orange by mounting flames. "My God," he whispered.

McKay let the last of a belt go in three bone-jarring bursts and rounded savagely on Sloan. "You were on a boat on-station off Beirut in '82, weren't you?" Sloan nodded. "And you boys shelled the place. Whole city blocks went up—just like that."

He nodded at the burning hell of the motel. "This is what my war was like. It's what yours was like, too —only you didn't have to look at it. You were nice and snug in the belly of your ship, where you couldn't smell the bodies burn."

Duvall threw down his M-16 and sat bolt up like a prairie dog out of his hole. "Wait!" he screamed. "The back of the motel! We're not guarding the back!"

With the bravery of desperation or just plain pissed-off, some of the PFs had come boiling out of the motel and were lying behind their parked vehicles busting caps. A man standing to Duvall's left blasting away from the hip went down shrieking as a 5.56 round tumbled like a chainsaw through his guts. The curly-haired leader never blinked.

"You just think of that?" McKay asked blandly.

"Some of them will get away!"

"Who gives a shit? Christ, somebody's got to get away to spread the word on how *baaad* we are . . ."

He was blowing his breath to no good end. Duvall grabbed his rifle and hopped up. "Follow me!" he shrieked, his voice drowning the howls of the gut-shot man. "We have to cut the bastards off!" And he was off and running.

Or thought he was. McKay shot straight out in a horizontal dive like a bolt out of a crossbow and tackled him by the legs as a burst of automatic fire crackled over their heads. "Slow down, asshole. You wanna get your head blown off?"

Duvall writhed in the bigger man's grip. "Let me go, damn you! We can't let them escape."

"That's the *idea*, dickbreath." Duvall's wiry body jackknifed. For a moment it looked as if he'd eel out of McKay's grip. Then the ex-marine got him by the back of his neck and ground his face into the cement-hard earth and clumps of wiry scrub grass.

For all the noise and fire the explosions had made, a fair number of the PFs had made it out by now, and while most of them were heading for the hills more than a few were firing back at the guerrillas' muzzle flashes. Somebody got to the Minimi machine gun in the improvised mount on the roll bar of an open jeep and began raking the scrub with it.

"We're pulling back, now," McKay said in Duvall's ear. "I just saved your ass. I ain't gonna do it again." He held the man a moment more, then let him go.

He crawled back to where Sloan was still lying next to the Maremont. "Dumb motherfucker," he said as Duvall picked himself up to a crouch, gave McKay a hot-eyed look, then gathered up his rifle and joined his comrades doing a quick fade into the darkened desert.

McKay shook his head. "Don't know how Tom put up with 'em, all those years in the Green Beanies. That's one fool gonna get himself and a lot of other people killed someday. If I had brain cell one I'd grease him myself."

He grabbed the Maremont and slapped Sloan on the

shoulder. "Let's book, Navy boy."

Sam wasn't the only one having a crisis of conscience that night.

Tom Rogers came back from a turn around the V-450, parked down the flank of a little round hill, to find Casey Wilson out of his bedroll, sitting with his back to one of the huge cleated tires.

"I can't sleep, man," the former fighter pilot explained.

Rogers picked up the clacker, the little hand detonator named for the sound it would make as it set off the four claymore mines arranged in a swastika around the vehicle. He clambered up on the front glacis of the armored car and sat with his rifle across his lap and the clacker held idly in one hand.

"What's the matter?" he asked. Unhurriedly, his expressionless gray eyes swept the surrounding hills. They were laagered down in the dry desert hills northeast of L.A. Before the war nothing much came this way but scorpions and the Manson Family, but these days you never could tell.

Casey bit his lips. His knees were drawn up to his chin. "I can't help thinking. About those men today. We must have killed a lot of them."

"Yeah."

The younger man shook his head. "It doesn't seem right somehow. I mean, they never had a chance!"

"There were a lot of them there, Case. How much chance would we have had in a fair fight?"

Casey said nothing.

"I know you hate the thought of having the expeditionary force in California," Tom said, softer than usual.

"I do. But still—" Casey shook his head again.

"They were just out there doing calisthenics, man. It doesn't seem right. They weren't *doing* anything."

"But they were. They were occupying American soil. Every minute, every day. It's our job to make them move. What we did today will make them feel a lot less comfortable hanging around."

"I know, Tom. It's just the thought of blowing all those helpless people up that gets to me. I'm used to fighting one-on-one."

Tom shrugged. "It's our job."

Casey looked at him. "You can be pretty cold sometimes, man."

Tom shrugged again.

Casey grimaced and stood. "Hey, man, I'm sorry. I didn't mean any offense. I was just, like, shooting my mouth off."

Rogers looked at him with a hint of puzzled frown. He hadn't taken any offense at his teammate's words. He accepted them as literal truth.

Casey leaned over and picked up his sniper's rifle, lying on its cordura case on the ground. "Go ahead and knock off, Tom," he said. "I don't think I'm, like, going to be able to sleep much tonight anyway."

CHAPTER
ELEVEN ─────────────────

McKay was just scraping the last of his breakfast
—some kind of scarfed bean soup that tasted the way
the camels smelled at the zoo, with a bit of boiled rabbit
stirred up inside—out of the can with a plastic spoon
when a kid scout came dusting up on a dirt bike. Sloan,
who'd been doing stretching exercises on the ground
next to the command jeep, stood up moving his arms in
slow circles. They were in an apple orchard up toward
the north end of the San Joaquin Valley. The sweet
smell of fallen apples, decomposing soft and orange-
brown on the ground, surrounded them like mist.

"Davey," Sloan said with a polite nod. "What can
we do for you?"

The towheaded youth skidded to a broadside stop
among the trees and flipped up his goggles. Trail dust
had caked on his face so that he resembled a negative-
image raccoon.

"Lieutenant McKay, Commander Sam," he shouted.

"You better come quick. Phil's in town, and he's sh-shooting people!"

McKay and Sloan looked at each other. "Shit," they exclaimed in unison, and grabbing up their weapons piled into the open Mazda four-wheel-drive.

They had been trying to operate without raising too much of a fuss for the moment. They had intelligence from their friends at Vista that an Effsee flying column with armor was working the region south of Modesto, trying to kick up enough dust that people wouldn't get the idea the military government's move from Sacramento south had been a scuttle.

The problem was, the whiz kids couldn't give McKay and Sloan any hard intelligence as to the whereabouts of the expeditionary force unit. While they owned the satellite network that carried FSE communications between the command in California and Europe, communications between Maitland's command and units on the ground in California went over telephone or surface radio, and were much dicier to intercept. So McKay had hoped to tread a bit lightly until they figured out just where the Effsee column was.

"Davey must be exaggerating," Sloan said from behind the wheel of the Mazda. His oblong face was pale beneath the tan that he, like the other Guardians, had been working up during their two weeks in California. "Duvall would never do anything as extreme as start executing people in town."

"Dream on," McKay grunted. He sat next to Sloan with his M-60 lightweight held up by the pistol grip and a cigar stuck in his face, streaming smoke like a thin blue pennon as the four-wheeler bounced down the dirt road toward the town near which they'd camped. "Duvall's a nut. And he's been getting too damn big for his britches."

General Maitland may have been taking steps to ensure people didn't see the military government's move as a scuttle, but they did anyway. The perception brought people out of the woodwork to join the resistance movement. There were all kinds: law-enforcement types sick of being coopted into oppressing their own neighbors, Effsee deserters, survivors looking to do what they could to make sure the withdrawing forces stayed headed in the right direction. Even a bunch of former Coast Guard types had turned up, whom Sam had promptly gotten hooked up with Lori and Donna and their crew, to start working on a plan to do something about the pirate threat.

But the apparent collapse of Effsee authority in the North had brought a lot of worms out into the light. Crooks and crazies and cardboard heroes who thought toting a gun was a great and splendid thing when it looked as if there wouldn't be many people in position to shoot back. People with scores to settle, people with hard-ons for the world in general, people who'd been hungering all their lives for the chance to let out somebody else's blood to see what it really looked like.

From a fairly compact guerrilla unit McKay and Sloan's team had swelled to over fifty, and McKay figured altogether too many of the new arrivals for whackos. What to do about them was another question entirely.

Duvall, that greasy little cocksucker, welcomed them. He envisioned the newcomers as increasing his own importance. And McKay was not ecstatic at the prospect of turning armed looneytunes loose to wander their backfield. At least if they stayed with the group he could keep an eye on them.

I was a dumb sonofabitch to send Tom south with Casey, he thought, as the Mazda jounced up the last hill before the small farming town near which they'd camped. *I shoulda gone myself, left Tom here.* He *knows how to deal with assholes like this.*

They topped the hill just in time to hear the Fourth-of-July popping of an M-16 on full auto. Sloan and McKay looked at each other, their mouths set hard. If Duvall had gotten to the point where he felt he could afford to ignore his "advisors" . . .

They went bombing down the slope as fast as Sloan could drive, and while he wasn't Casey Wilson he did have incentive. Young Davey the scout from San Jose came fishtailing behind them on his Honda.

Hardin was the usual collection of gas stations and whitewashed churches, bars and convenience stores, funky old frame houses and some stucco boxes of more recent vintage, with a used-car lot on one side of town and a yard on the other filled with brightly colored heavy farm equipment nobody'd been able to afford for years before the One-Day War. A megatonner going off near Frisco had blistered some paint on the western faces of a few buildings, busted some picture windows, injured a few people, but the war itself hadn't hit the little town nestled among pleasant rolling hills very hard. Since then Hardin had had its ups and downs like everyplace else: refugees, plague, marauders—some in uniform and others strictly private operations. By and large the survivors carried on, like millions of others the world around.

More shots popped from the center of town as the Mazda roared past Diablo Used Cars, the Sleepy Hollow Trailer Park and the Dew Drop Inn. McKay checked the half-moon Australian ammo box clipped onto the M-60's receiver.

The center of town was just a few blocks beyond the outskirts. A brick town hall faced a little park planted with shade trees. It was all as neat and sweet as something from some nostalgia flick about the 1950s, except for the crowd of nervous townspeople herded together in front of the municipal building under the eyes of a score of guerrillas with rags around their heads and careless grips on their liberated automatic weapons, and the half-dozen bodies lying in the middle of a darker stain on the dark asphalt in front of the wide cement steps.

Phil Duvall stood on the cement pier next to the steps, with one waffle-stomper propped on a basketball-sized cement sphere. He had on black jeans and a blue denim shirt open at the throat to show off a spray of the curly black hair on his chest. He had a Heckler & Koch Model 91 assault rifle hanging around his neck on an Israeli-style sling just like the ones the Guardians used.

A washed-out-looking blond woman was tearing at the hard hands which held a bearded man in greasy mechanic's coveralls by the elbows. "We had to work for the Effsees," she was shouting up at Duvall through her tears. "They'd have shot us if we didn't cooperate."

Duvall set his narrow jaw and shook his head. "We're at war. War calls for sacrifices. You should have spat in the fascists' faces!"

"They'd have killed us!" the woman screamed.

"Now we're gonna kill you," said one of the burly kids holding her husband, "so it all works out the same, don't it."

Several of Duvall's armed hangers-on arranged around the town hall steps guffawed appreciatively. Sloan braked to a stop halfway down the block. Some of the townpeople glanced toward them, but most just stared at Duvall as if he were their favorite soap opera.

"We seem to be breaking up a lot of lynch mobs these days," McKay remarked, standing up in the front seat of the open-topped vehicle. He hefted the Maremont and blasted out three of the town hall's second-story windows with a quick burst.

Resistance heroes went in all directions. Duvall stood

his ground, though broken glass dusted his shoulders and shaggy hair like snow. "What the hell are you doing?" he shouted.

"We might ask you the same question," Sloan called back. He had picked up his Galil assault rifle with the fat M-203 grenade launcher fixed underneath. He wasn't pointing it at anything in particular. Yet.

"Handing out justice to traitors!" yelled the second burly kid who had hold of the guy in coveralls. He and his buddy were picking themselves and their unfortunate captive up off the street.

"Looks a lot like murder to me," McKay said, his voice reverberating off the storefronts. "And don't point that thing at me, you sniveling little puke, or I'll punch you a half dozen new assholes."

He swung the M-60's muzzle to bear on a kid who was fidgeting with his rifle behind Duvall. The defiance dropped right off the youngster's face and he almost fumbled his weapon in his abrupt eagerness to point it somewhere else.

Duvall looked petulant. "You shouldn't interfere. This is our state. It's our business. Not yours."

McKay laughed. "Yeah, I noticed how you was takin' care of business before we arrived. You never even had the balls to start shooting unarmed civilians until we turned up."

Most of Duvall's guerrillas had now emerged from the cover they'd dived into when McKay cut loose. They were muttering among themselves in an ugly way, casting sidelong glances at the two men in the Mazda. It was clear they weren't happy at having their game interrupted. But they'd seen the M-60 and Sloan's grenade launcher in action. Nobody wanted to be first to make a play at the Guardians.

"I think it's time you got busted to the ranks, Duvall," McKay told the partisan leader, whose face had turned an ugly brownish-red.

"Like fuck!" Duvall screamed. "These are my men! They follow me, not you—you outsiders."

A scream cut the sky in half and the front blew off the Wendy's across the park. "Incoming!" shouted somebody who'd either seen action or a shitload of war movies, as the noise of the blast echoed off the bluffs behind the town.

A second explosion off to the Guardians' right tossed debris into sight above the town hall.

"We have got a serious problem here," McKay observed.

"Mortars," Sloan said. "Well, now we know where the Effsee column is."

About half of Duvall's loyal followers were booking for the bluffs just as fast as their little legs could carry them while Duvall shrieked obscenities after them. The others stared wildly in all directions but held their ground while the townsfolk scattered.

"Look up there!" one of the guerrillas yelled. He pointed an arm encased in K mart cammies to the wooded hill that rose half a klick northwest of town, past which the main street ran after it turned back into a county road.

A long black tube came poking out of the trees. Then a tree trunk split with a rippling crack, and the rest of an M-60 tank came waddling into plain view.

A jagged chunk of fire gushed from the cannon, and an alcohol-burning panel truck blew up across the plaza. The sound of that explosion reached the Guardians the same instant as the roar of the shot. Even at this range they felt the quick push of overpressure from the muzzle blast.

Other armored vehicles were now appearing over the hill, boxy M-113 armored personnel carriers with the blue-and-white FSE insignia painted on their bows.

Their tailgates dropped and troops began to spill out as the APC commanders hosed heavy-caliber ball ammo into the town from machine guns mounted in their cupolas.

Duvall was shouting orders. More and more of his frontline fighters were doing that time-honored bug-out boogie, but he seemed to be trying to whip the others forward in a counterattack.

"What an asshole," McKay said. He dropped the Maremont and picked up a long, evil-looking RPG-7V and a Kelty daypack stuffed with three reloads from the Mazda's back seat. "Get the hell out of town," he said to Sloan. "Try to rally the survivors on the bluffs. I'm gonna see if I can slow these suckers up for a few minutes."

He bailed out as Duvall jogged past, leading six or seven guerrillas just as whacked-out on hatred as he was. Or maybe they'd seen too many Sylvester Stallone flicks and figured themselves bulletproof. Sloan sat gaping at McKay with one hand on the wheel and the other still clutching his Galil.

"Clear out!" McKay bellowed. "I ain't playing hero. *Trust* me."

Sloan gunned the engine and laid rubber up the block, almost lost it when he swerved to miss the victims of Duvall's drum-head court martial, and went zipping out of town.

McKay ran at an angle to the route taken by the guerrillas—he didn't even want to be *anywhere* nearby when they started busting caps and calling lots of attention to themselves. He was jogging down a side street when Davey came buzzing up on his dirt bike, face flushed behind his goggles.

"Go back!" McKay waved a frantic arm at the boy. "This ain't anyplace for you."

"I want to go with you," the boy called back.

McKay shook his head and ran on.

Up on the wooded hill an APC commander spotted two figures moving along a street near the edge of town, swept it with .50-caliber fire. A couple of big bullets hit Davey and sent him bouncing off his bike and back down the block like a tumbleweed blown in a hot Santa Ana wind.

McKay ducked into the parking lot behind a mom and pop hardware store that state and federal regulations had somehow failed to shut down. The .50-caliber bullets went right through the brick building, sending pink-gray dust cascading down on McKay as he hugged the pavement, but the APC boy was firing blind, and quickly lost interest.

McKay glanced at the street. Davey lay there on his back looking at the sky, his body arranged in that aimless sort of sprawl reserved for discarded dolls and dead people. McKay grimaced. The kid had been fifteen. McKay picked up the rocket launcher, dodged to the next street over, and ran on.

In a couple of minutes he found himself in the backyard of a ranch-style brick house, with a portable barbecue moldering away still on the concrete patio. McKay squatted down behind a large doghouse peeling turquoise paint like dead skin and took a peek.

A hundred or so troopies in battle dress were halfway to the town. Most of them had American uniforms and M-16s, though some looked like British Army and carried bullpup AUG assault rifles. The M-60 was puttering along behind them, spitting shells into the town at apparent random. The air was thick with the stink of diesel fuel and burned explosives and burning suburbia.

To McKay's right a storm of fire broke out of a frame farmhouse. A couple of khaki-clad Limeys went down, and then the rest of the advancing line went to earth and began to shoot back. McKay made himself small. In military parlance the plywood doghouse offered concealment but not cover, which meant the bad guys could shoot right through it even with small arms, but they couldn't see him if he played his cards right. He set the daypack with the three spare rockets down and readied the Soviet-made antitank launcher.

A grenade launcher coughed, and screams erupted from the farmhouse. Tendrils of dense white smoke came writhing like snakes out the windows—the Guardians weren't the only people who ever heard of white phosphorus. In a moment Phil Duvall raced out the back door with his hair and denim workshirt smoldering, firing from the hip.

The tank's main gun ejaculated flame. Duvall vanished in an orange explosion. Half a minute later another 105-mm round blew half the farmhouse apart. The soldiers stood and advanced again.

McKay brought himself to a kneeling position and set the launcher on his shoulder. If he could fuck up the tank he would take a good deal of steam out of this assault. Having a big iron dinosaur to back them up made troops feel invulnerable; if anything happened to their guardian dragon, on the other hand, they suddenly felt small and weak and generally doomed. It wouldn't stop them, but it might slow them up enough to let most of the guerrillas get away.

McKay squinted through the optical sight. The M-60 was 220 meters away, a longish shot for the RPG-7 in spite of what its manufacturers claimed. On the other hand it wasn't moving very fast. And it was a *big* target.

He aimed for the base of the turret. The rocket-propelled grenade, which resembled two fat ice cream cones stuck together at their big ends, had enough kick to bust an M-60's front armor. But the turret-base was especially vulnerable, and any penetration at all would set fire to the highly inflammable hydraulic fluid, practically ensuring a kill. When it came to going one-on-one with sixty-four tons of tank, Billy McKay believed in riding any advantage he could catch.

The M-60 lumbered forward at a few klicks an hour, just pacing the advancing troops. Machine-gun fire from the M-113s on the hill cracked over McKay's head like thunder. Mortars slammed like giant doors.

He pressed the trigger.

The rocket flew true on a plume of white smoke, buzzing like a huge horsefly. It hit the turret ring to the left of the main gun's shroud, just where he'd aimed it, and went thud.

" 'Thud'?" Billy McKay echoed. Old soldier that he was, he knew that a shaped-charge warhead blasting death into the vitals of an armored fighting vehicle did not go *thud*.

He'd scored a bull's-eye with a dud round.

"Russian piece of shit." He clutched frantically for the pack. But the tank commander, sitting half out of the turret, had seen the telltale smoke puff of the launch, and was pointing a gauntleted hand right at McKay's personal doghouse. That long, wicked cannon was swinging to bear with surprising speed.

"Fuck *me*," McKay said. He threw away the launcher and ran like a bunny.

Behind him the doghouse blew up. The blast threw him over a chain-link fence and into oblivion.

He was starting to hear his own voice mumbling obscenities by the time he dragged himself up to the top of the bluff. He reached for a conveniently protruding root, and almost shit his largely nonexistent pants when a strong hand caught him by the wrist.

"We were about to go looking for you," Sam Sloan grunted as he hauled him up over the lip with a strength McKay tended to forget he possessed. "Then we heard you crunching and swearing your way up through the bushes.''

McKay lay on his back and panted through blistered lips.

Sloan stood up and studied him with his hands on his hips. "You've never been pretty, McKay, but now you're fit to frighten small children."

"Thanks too fucking much." The words sounded as if they were being spoken in the next room of a cheap apartment. Come to think of it, McKay had lived places where he could hear better through the walls. "What the hell do you expect me to look like? I just been blown up."

Perverse as explosions always were, the shell burst hadn't torn him apart, but it had blown one leg off his camouflaged pants and slashed the upper half of his coveralls like a punker's T-shirt, and the flash had seared him here and there. All in all he looked like death refried. Which was just how he felt.

"I can't tell you how much goddam fun it is playing hide and seek with half a company of legs when you can't hear and feel like you're walking underwater," he said.

"Glad you made it."

A number of Duvall's raiders had clustered around curiously, making sure the bushes hid them from view of the town. The savage suddenness of the Effsee attack seemed to have made them forget all about their mad with the Guardians.

"Where's Phil?" somebody asked.

"Blown into itty-bitty fucking pieces. Somebody get me some field glasses. I gotta see what's going on in town."

A round-faced Hispanic with a mustache and an Army jacket he might actually have been entitled to wear brought a pair from the Mazda. McKay crawled around to a point overlooking the center of town and bellied up to the edge of the cliff.

Soldiers were moving around in the town. The occasional bang of a grenade, inevitably followed by a quick snarl of automatic fire, testified that the FSE troops were still mopping up imaginary resistance. Others were prodding the long-suffering townsfolk back into the park before the town hall at gunpoint.

As McKay watched, an open command car came charging down the main drag and fishtailed to a stop in front of the brick municipal building. A big red-faced man in American uniform got out. He had a pair of .45 automatics on his hips and a riding crop under his arm. His helmet looked chromed.

"I wish to hell they'd never made *Patton*," McKay said.

He focused on the unit patch on the man's upper arm as he mounted the pier where Duvall had stood not an hour before. It sported the dark red triangle with the rounded corners and base that was the distinctive badge of the 123rd Infantry Division, United States Army.

McKay groaned. "The Dickheads! We had our asses whipped by the Dickheads. I can't take it."

He slithered back. "I've seen enough. Let's book while the booking is good."

"Ladies and gentlemen of Hardin," the bulky, florid officer said in an orator's long-ranged voice, "I am Colonel J. R. Ramsay of the United States Army, serving with the Federated States of Europe expeditionary force. Serving with pride, I can tell you."

He stood with his riding crop gripped behind the leather-reinforced seat of his jodhpurs, bouncing slightly on the balls of his feet. The townsfolk looked up at him silently. He could feel their fear and awe swelling inside him.

He didn't look much like George C. Scott, to say nothing of George S. Patton, Jr., although he kept on trying. He was a tall man in his late forties who had kept himself in decent shape. But his jowls sagged a bit too much to either side of his chin, his eyes were on the piggy side, his nose was shapeless rather than craggy, and his face seemed to collapse in the center, as if his dentures didn't fit quite right. He thought of himself as Piledriver—Piledriver Ramsay, that was it, and actually believed his men thought of him the same way. They didn't. Though their names for him were just as picturesque.

In the years before the One-Day War the 123rd had earned a reputation as the saddest-sack outfit in the U.S. Army, if not the NATO alliance. Its nickname actually sprang from its peculiar divisional patch, but was universally held to be appropriate. And among the forces on the ground in Europe, J. R. Ramsay had earned renown as the Ultimate Dickhead.

"I see before me," he bellowed, pointing the end of his riding crop at the bodies in the street, "evidence of the lawless anarchy which has gripped this country since the Third World War. The expeditionary force came to this country to restore law and order. That it shall do.

"Some may think the removal of the military government from Sacramento is a sign we're withdrawing. Nothing could be further from the truth. And the 522nd Battalion of the FSE expeditionary force is here to prove it. Now, who was responsible for this atrocity?"

Nobody answered. Ramsay's face began to turn purple, and he made frog noises down in the depths of his thick neck. The cordoning soldiers prodded the citizens with their rifles.

After a moment a stoutish man with gray-blond whiskers, wearing gray trousers and vest and a blue silk tie, was surreptitiously elbowed forward by his neighbors.

"Ah," the Piledriver said. "And who might you be, sir?"

The man in two-thirds of a three-piece was scowling back over alternate shoulders. "Uh, Talbot, Colonel. Willis Talbot. I'm, ah, I'm the mayor of Hardin."

"I see. And who committed these murders?"

"Guerrillas. They, they ran away when you opened fire." He waved a manicured hand at the front of the town hall. "It was terrible, Colonel. They were vandals, crazy mad. They shot out all the windows."

Meanwhile a second figure had climbed out of the back seat of Ramsay's command car and ambled up to stand on the steps, near the colonel but not too near. It was a small man with silver-gray hair combed lankly over a prominent bald spot and eyes like obsidian buttons set to either side of a fleshy, wet-looking nose. A white stubble of beard furred his cheeks. He wore a green-turquoise shirt with exaggerated collar points under an orange-russet leisure suit. The shirt collar was discolored where it rubbed his scrawny neck, and there were grease spots scattered here and there down the front of his jacket.

Now Ramsay tipped his head to the left and said from the corner of his mouth, "He's lying. This town is full of collaborators. I can smell them."

The man took an ancient Baby Ruth candy bar from his pocket, peeled it, bit into it. The stale candy made a noise like a breaking branch. "Naw," he said. "They're telling the truth. These guerrilla types can't resist playing big shot. Coming into town, firing their guns off, showing what big balls they have. Don't mean diddly shit."

Ramsay frowned at him. Maitland's G-2 had insisted

the man was the expert on conditions in the North. Ramsay lacked faith in him. He resembled a largish rat, for one thing. For another, there was that *smell* . . .

"Mr. Baxter," he said in a low voice, "your naivete amazes me."

Baxter shrugged and stuffed the rest of the candy bar in his face. Half the wrapper went with it. He chomped away with his mouth open.

"Very well, Mr. Mayor," Ramsay said, turning hurriedly back and projecting again. "You consider yourself a loyal American, do you not?"

"Uh, yes. I mean, of course I am."

"Then you'll no doubt be happy to cooperate by pointing out all those subversive elements who cooperated with the traitorous bandits we just drove from your town. And while you're at it, you might point out the various black-marketeers and profiteers hiding in your midst."

Talbot looked blank. "Why?"

"Why, so we can shoot them, of course." Ramsay slapped his shanks with his riding crop and beamed. "We're going to give this town just the medicine it needs: a dose of good old-fashioned discipline."

"Dickhead," Baxter said. But he said it softly, and the wad of paper and rock-hard candy in his mouth garbled it into unintelligibility.

"What's that, Mr. Baxter?"

"Nothing."

CHAPTER
TWELVE ———————————

For a week Piledriver Ramsay and the 522nd Battalion (Mixed) had it all their way. They rampaged around, handing out doses of firing-squad discipline liberally to the civilian populace. They wiped out two small settlements tied into Morgenstern's network: a survivalists' retreat for harboring guerrillas, and a peaceful commune on the coast for black-market activities and smuggling.

The Guardians tried to keep them off-balance. Even McKay was reluctant to expose American civilians to reprisal killings, but Ramsay was so enthusiastic about shooting people that McKay figured not too many more would suffer if the guerrillas put pressure on the Effsees. And Ramsay's iron-fist tactics worked the way that approach always does: a bunch of people were cowed into helping the occupying forces or at least not hindering them—and a bunch who earlier didn't give much of a damn suddenly had very personal reasons for throwing in with the rebels. It balanced for the most part, but Tom, who had just returned from Southern California, said they were getting the better of it in the long run, and he had a master's eye for these things.

The guerrillas went out in small groups to hassle Ramsay's battalion—which as far as the Guardians could tell was more an overcharged company, but the Effsees loved to put grand names on things—bush-whacking patrols, firing up supply convoys, and the old Vietcong favorite, lobbing rockets at random into their encampments after dark.

The spectacular demise of Phil Duvall had made a lot of the crazier elements think better about playing Che Guevara in the California hills. The stocky and mustached feminist Martha Gambatelli now led the largest bunch, and no matter how prejudiced McKay was against broads with guns he had to admit she was a lot smarter—and tougher, when you got right down to it—than the fanatical Duvall had ever been.

The other really solid strike force was the Red Baron's commie heroes. Like just about all the domestic communists McKay had ever met, the People's Republic of the Bear boys were almost exclusively from the sheltered middle classes—and McKay could tell, since his own collar was as blue as they get—but they were tough, smart bastards. McKay secretly kind of hoped they all got to be commie martyrs before the Effsees were dealt with. Otherwise the Guardians were going to have to cope with them themselves.

It was a damn good thing their old buddy Ivan Vesensky, late of the KGB and now Yevgeny Maximov's head mischief-maker at large, had headed east to try to pry the Guardians out of Washington. Vesensky operated in the Soviet tradition, which was to say he welcomed all allies who might be useful, regardless of belief—

ideology had played no role in Soviet policy for half a century. Since his departure the MilGov's head, General Maitland, had followed his natural inclination and pissed-off all the leftist terrorist groups Vesensky had managed to keep in harness after the van Damm debacle. At the same time, Maitland favored the right-wing loons, Reverend Forrie Smith's faithful listeners for the most part, who flocked to the Effsee flag, fleshing out his well-loved popular forces with them.

That made McKay happy too. Having to stomach Ku Kluxers as well as commie bastards would have been too damn much.

But when rebel forces and the Effsees brushed up against each other the guerrillas tended to get their noses bloodied. The 522nd wasn't all Dickheads. There were troops from American units which hadn't run away quite so fast when the balloon went up in Europe, or at all. And some of the Limeys were pretty hard-core. Ramsay was a nickel-plated hemorrhoid, but he had a strak fighting force to play with.

On the other hand, Tom Rogers was now back from his flying recce of Southern California, and McKay figured that meant the tide had turned . . .

"What's for breakfast?" McKay asked, hauling himself to a sitting position on the sleeping mat. He regretted it at once; the hardwood floor seemed to slam against his tailbone. "Jesus. These fucking futons were never meant for white men."

"Good, healthy fruit," said the tall lean woman in the Mexican peasant shirt and jeans and with a braided leather band tied around the temples of her gray-dusted black hair. She held up a plate covered with a white cloth.

McKay groaned and lay back with his eyes shut. The

almost-rhythmic banging of a windmill outside filled the room and buzzed in McKay's bones like overamped bass. Morning light filtered in through the walls as well as the curtained window, strangely colored by the fiberglass panels that made up the geodesic dome that was the house.

"How about something a man can get his teeth into? Whatever happened to ham and eggs?"

"We don't believe in abusing our bodies with animal products, nor in killing our animal friends so we can stuff ourselves with their flesh," she said, kneeling to place the plate beside McKay's bed. "Fruit gives our bodies all they need to thrive." She spoke without heat; this same debate had gone on every morning for a week.

"There's mint tea, too," she said, setting down an earthenware pot with a Japanese-style cup hanging upturned on the spout. She left.

"But it tastes like goddam mouthwash," McKay called after her as the beaded curtains rattled down into place behind her. To make things worse she had a fanny like a board.

"Hearts and minds, McKay," said Sloan, pushing aside the bead strands with one finger. "How's our patient today?"

"Arrgh," McKay said. He had a shell splinter in his ankle, which didn't seem likely to do any permanent damage but made him limp, plus assorted bruises and contusions. Worse, he'd gotten concussed when the shell burst knocked him out, and kept having spells of dizziness and nausea. Rogers insisted he stay inactive and under observation for at least a week. For a man with nerves of Portland cement Tom Rogers was a total pussy when it came to his teammates' health. Any little thing went wrong with them, and he went into Jewish-mother mode.

But it was the commune they'd wound up going to ground in, not far from Coalinga, that made it toughest to bear. McKay would have preferred shacking up at Vista, but they couldn't risk compromising their bone-vital line plugged into the main artery of FSE communications. And the crew here were not McKay's kind of people at all. All the women were skinny and claimed to be under vows of celibacy. Maybe it was just the way he asked.

"These fruitbars are trying to starve me, Sam," McKay said, fluttering a hand the size of an entrenching tool weakly at the covered plate.

"They're fruitarians, McKay. Jesus."

"Yeah. I'd be better off with fruitbars at that. *They* got no silly prejudice against protein. Otherwise, how the hell would they—"

"McKay!"

McKay took a plum from the plate and eyed it without favor. "What word from the front?"

"Morgenstern's people picked up those injured men."

McKay scowled. One of the joint PRB/Sons of Hayduke teams had gotten slammed hard by an Effsee patrol in the woods on Highway 1 near Lucia. Its leader reported a couple of casualties in need of major medical treatment—which meant the best they had to look forward to was 120 grains of copper-jacketed lead for anesthetic, applied to the back of the neck. One of the ugly realities of life after the holocaust.

Then to everybody's surprise Morgenstern himself had called in to offer to collect the two for emergency treatment. Among the Project Blueprint heavyweights he'd gathered at his hideout was a top-flight surgeon or two, it seemed. McKay hated to risk blowing the hideout's location—*he* didn't even know where it was, for

Chrissake—but Morgenstern said his own people would make the pickup, and the injured could be blindfolded. McKay agreed, as he had no illusions that he could forbid the crusty Israeli economist to do anything that came into his head.

Tom came in with his Kevlar-sided medical case, flipped up the lid, and booted up the built-in computer. "Time for vital-signs check."

"I got kwashiorkor from no goddam protein. Also beri-beri from not enough vitamin B."

"Every morning you get a shot with enough vitamins to make a bronze statue of Robert E. Lee start slam-dancing," Sloan pointed out. "I know because you bellow like a branded bull-calf every time you get it."

"That's because Clara Barton here uses a needle the size of a drill bit."

"I have to, to get through that thick hide of yours," said Rogers.

McKay and Sloan gaped at the medic. "That's his joke for the year," McKay said around a thermometer. "We're safe now."

Rogers checked the LCD screen and plucked the thermometer out.

"How's Casey?" McKay asked.

Rogers shrugged. "Moping around somewhere. I'll talk to him."

Casey had been back in his funk since his jaunt to L.A. with Tom. The war had come home for him in a way it never had before.

Several weeks before a mixed unit of American Effsee regulars and PFs had paid a visit to Balin's Forge in Simi Valley north of Los Angeles. Balin had been out on a salvage run with Lancelot and Idaho, which was fortunate. The popular force accused the Forge crew of looting. Balin's wife Jeannie had protested. One thing

led to another. Jeannie got roughed up. Young Lonny
Chin got hauled off to some kind of detention camp,
and Shep the cook got dead. And tall, redheaded
Rhoda, Casey Wilson's lover, had been dragged into a
back room for some old-fashioned gang rape.

Though Casey never said so, even to his buddies, he
surmised Jeannie had been raped too. He knew that it
had happened to her before, when she was thirteen. It
wasn't the sort of thing you got used to, but she could
deal with it. And if she had been, she hid the fact; it was
all they could do to keep Balin from rushing over to PF
headquarters and getting gunned down as it was.

That was why Lancelot and Idaho had been so
guarded at the meeting in San Ramon. The Effsees had
never been back, despite their threats to return and
clean the Forge out for good. But Balin had stayed
drunk ever since.

And Rhoda had been shattered. She was a naive kid,
a middle-class L.A. suburbanite in whose world things
like that did not happen, another waif taken in after the
big blow-up by Balin and his wife. She refused even to
see Casey at first.

There was nothing he could do to heal her. He could
try to reassure her of her own worth, and he did. How
much it worked he couldn't tell. The experience filled
him with a sensation he'd never known, of impotence,
of helplessness—and no matter how laid-back and mel-
low he acted, he was still at core a fighter jock who did
not deal with helplessness well. He was hit as hard by his
inability to think of any way to help his lover and friend
as by what had happened to her.

And the whole nasty mess had brought another unfamiliar emotion to him: anger. Anger that hated and
went straight to the marrow like a bone-seeker. Never
again would he feel the slightest compunction about

blowing unsuspecting Effsees to bloody screaming rags on their own parade ground. For the first time in his life he felt he had a score to settle.

"He'll get over it," McKay said. It sounded unfeeling. But in the bared-blade world the Guardians inhabited—that everyone inhabited, these days—you had to learn to put compassion and sorrow aside. Otherwise you died. And Casey was a survivor, like the rest of them.

"Well, everything checks out," Rogers remarked, closing his case with a snap. "I reckon you can return to active status." He frowned, rubbed his scarred chin. "Also, I think you should get some meals from Mobile One's store. You do need more protein than you been getting."

McKay sat up and spread his arms. "I get to eat meat again? Tom, come here and let me kiss you!"

"Maybe you would be more at home among the fruit-bars, McKay," Sloan said. He scowled. "I don't believe I just said that."

"Excuse me," said a voice from the doorway.

An apologetic face shielded behind huge wire-rimmed glasses had poked through the bead curtain.

"Come on in, Andy," Sloan said. "We're all friends here."

Magnified blue eyes blinked behind thick lenses. "Excuse me," the fruitarian said again, "but there seems to be a tank in our front yard."

Six eyes gave the young man their undivided attention. "Say what?" McKay said after a moment.

"I said, there's, uh, a tank. Out front."

Sloan laughed. "I didn't know you were such a practical joker, Andy. You gave us quite a turn."

Andy looked as if he were about to bust into tears.

"Billy, Sam, Tom," Casey Wilson's voice whispered urgently in the Guardians' ears, "you better come quick. There's a tank out front of the house!"

Guardians went in all directions. Tom dashed out the rear of the dome to meet Casey and try to get into the big wooden shed where Mobile One was concealed unobserved. Sloan went out the back and headed for the trees, hoping for a flank shot at the tank—the HEDP armor-piercing rounds his M-203 fired didn't have much chance against a tank's frontal armor. It didn't have much chance against the side armor, either, but he couldn't be too choosey.

Carrying his Maremont, twenty pounds of black iron which suddenly felt every bit as powerful as a twist of pink cotton candy, McKay walked to the front door in his cammie trousers and undershirt.

Casey was right. There was a tank in the front yard. An M-60 with an old-style 105-mm gun, just like the one he'd bounced the rocket off in the abortive battle of Hardin. It wasn't America's most modern main battle tank. But then, it didn't have to be.

He took a deep breath and stepped out into daylight.

The commander sitting half out of the turret wore British uniform, as did the driver who popped his head out of the hatch when McKay emerged. "I say," the commander said, "are you with the resistance chaps?"

No, señor, I am a peaceful farmer, McKay had a mad impulse to say. *And this here? It's a tractor differential.*

"Yeah," he said instead.

"Smashing," the driver said. He had red hair and was missing a tooth.

"We'd like to discuss surrender terms," the tank commander added.

"We ain't gonna surrender."

The Limey commander laughed. He had better teeth than the driver. "No, no. We wish to surrender to you."

McKay let the machine gun hang by its sling and dug at his ear with a finger. "Now, I thought I just heard you say—"

"We're throwin' in the bloody towel, mate," the driver said cheerfully. "But only if we can get decent terms, mind. No POW cages or any of that rubbish."

McKay noticed for the first time that the main gun was at full elevation and cranked way over so as not to bear on the gaudy dome. "Sam," he said, "I think you better come talk to these boys."

In a moment Sloan came strolling from the trees next to the dome with his Galil hanging on its sling. "Good morning, gentlemen. What exactly did you have in mind."

"Surrender," they told him.

"Why?"

"FS bloody E's givin' it up, ain't it?" the driver said, and spat. "Don't half fancy going back to Europe to let a bunch of dervishes carve on my private parts."

"*What did you say?*" McKay shouted.

"You hard of hearin', mate?" the driver inquired with interest.

"Orders came through this morning, old man," the commander said in his plummy public school accent. "The expeditionary force is withdrawing to help defend the Federated States against this Iskander chap."

"They're scarpering," the driver said. "Only we decided to do a bunk of our own. Better than putting up with that cunt Ramsay any longer."

"Tom," McKay subvocalized to his teammate, who had snuck into the shed and worked his way into Mobile

One's turret. Casey was fidgeting behind the V-450's wheel, in case spectacular suicide seemed to be in order. "Get on the horn to Vista pronto and find out what the fuck's going down."

"How did you find us?" Sloan wanted to know.

"Asked about the neighborhood for representatives of the resistance. People can be quite forthcoming when someone in a tank makes polite inquiry, don't you know."

The two Guardians were dumbfounded. "Why the hell didn't Ramsay find us, if it's so goddam easy?"

"Because he's a proper Charlie."

"Never thought to bleedin' ask, did he?" the driver said. "Never even listened to that grimy bugger Intelligence hung on him."

"Not that brother Baxter was the sort to inspire confidence," the commander murmured.

"Baxter!" Sloan and McKay shouted in unison.

The commander looked surprised. "Yes, that's the fellow's name. Little chap, rather resembles a rat, badly in need of a good steam-cleaning."

"Why, that slimy little piece of shit," McKay grunted.

"An apt description. But to get back to our surrender—"

"Billy, Sam," Tom's voice came, "Vista confirms. The *mujahideen* have pushed into Austria, and Chairman Maximov is calling his boys home in a hurry. The expeditionary force is withdrawing ASAP by way of San Diego."

Sam and Billy let out whoops, embraced each other, and began to jump up and down as if they'd just won the World Series.

"Maybe we should try to give up somewhere else,"

the tank driver said dubiously.

"No, no," Sloan said, releasing McKay. "What terms did you gentlemen have in mind?"

"We'd hoped to exchange the old battlewagon here for a tractor," the commander said.

"A tractor?"

"Too right," the driver said. "We want to form our own agricultural collective, don't we?"

CHAPTER
THIRTEEN ──────────

"You can't destroy the laboratory," Dr. Mahal-aby whispered in shock.

Lieutenant Dorn shivered slightly in his lightweight summer uniform. The sun was low in the western sky and the amber light it poured up the mountain valley wasn't enough to take the early October edge out of the mountain air.

"I'm sorry, Doctor. We have our orders."

"*Orders,*" Susan Spinelli said, her fine face twisting contemptuously. "What are you, Germans or Americans?"

"Americans, ma'am. Patriotic ones. Though we've got Germans serving in the expeditionary force as well. You should be grateful our allies have been willing to lend us a hand in our time of need." *But you aren't*, he thought bitterly. You couldn't even think of these people as traitors, that was the worst part of it. They really thought of the expeditionary force as interlopers, invaders. They didn't see that the country had fallen into anarchy, that only a firm hand could pull it out of that morass again. In his expeditionary force, the FSE's Chairman Maximov had extended such a hand.

And now that help was being withdrawn. All because of the same damned Muslim fanatics Dorn had fought in the Mideast, before he got rotated to Europe just in time for the Soviet incursion. And because of the resistance of misguided, well-meaning civilian idiots like the people of New Eden.

"You have taken our seeds," the Lebanese-born doctor said, wagging a shaggy paw at the semitrailer parked in front of the main habitat with its engine mumbling softly to itself. Its long silver box was packed full not just of the seeds of a dozen special food strains developed here, miraculously productive and resistant to disease and weather, but of samples and notes and floppy disks. Everything needed to enable agronomists in the FSE to duplicate the incredible feats achieved here in the commune-cum-lab called New Eden.

"Our special crops will enable you to feed the starving multitudes of Europe," Mahalaby said, "and welcome to it; we serve all humanity here. But surely, there's no reason to destroy what we have left. Think of what we can accomplish in the future!"

Wearily Dorn shook his head. He was a young man, very tall, not much meat on him, not exactly good-looking. Just another grunt trying to do what he thought was right.

"I'm sorry, Doctor. I truly am. I don't make the decisions—"

"But what will become of my people?" the enormous scientist wailed. His hairy cheeks were wet with tears, and Dorn was afraid for a moment the man would grab him. He hated to be touched by other people.

"I don't know," he said frankly, backing away. Beyond the slope of Mahalaby's shoulder he saw Susan Spinelli, her face drawn like an artist's canvas on its frame, glance over to four or five heavily armed civilians lounging around the tractor's cab. Some of the Donner clan's hired hands—which meant hired guns. They were looking at her and laughing.

Once the troops pulled out the Donners' lowlifes would be swarming all over this valley, that was sure. Maybe that was why the powers-that-be wanted the place trashed, though God knew Maitland or somebody seemed to love General Edwards, and that meant he and his allies the Donners were untouchable. Since coming here months ago Dorn had been under the strictest instructions to treat the loyal locals with kid gloves.

Distasteful as he found a lot of the stunts the people from the neighboring valley pulled, Dorn obeyed orders. Being too squeamish about the behavior of valuable allies had lost the Vietnam War, as far as Dorn was concerned, and shackled American policy ever since. But he had his limits. When Randy Donner, head of the family since his old man had kicked over the winter, had carried off one of Mahalaby's technicians for a bedwarmer, Dorn had wanted to bring her back by force. Sacramento nixed that; the most Dorn was permitted to do was inform the Donners to keep their hands off New Eden personnel in future, even if the lab was nominally under Edwards's authority.

Randy's fat little fuckwad of a brother, Buddy, had been casting his pig's eyes in the direction of the lissome Spinelli, but Dorn had faced him down. The lieutenant could see how the blond scientist viewed his imminent departure with alarm. *They've resented us every second we were here,* he thought. *Once we're gone, maybe they'll appreciate why we came in the first place.*

A drumroll of hoofbeats on hard earth brought his head around. Here was Randy Donner himself, a muscular young man with the heavy jaw and thick black eyebrows of a 1950s leading man, riding a big shiny bay. A smallish sleek man rode a dappled gray mare at his elbow. He had an immaculate air to him that belied his rugged outdoor dress.

"Mr. Donner, Mr. Halpern," the lieutenant said, nodding.

"Fred. Call me Fred, Lieutenant." The slick dude swung down from the mare as some of the loungers hopped forward to catch the reins. He was Edwards's right-hand man, had been since the general retired from the Air Force to enter politics, some years before the war. Donner dismounted more leisurely behind him. "I understand you're planning to destroy this facility. Certainly, if that's just an idle rumor—"

"It's not."

Halpern's lips set in his plumpish face. He had a sort of taut softness to him, like a well-stuffed satin cushion. His smell of vaguely scented soap overrode even the stink of diesel and horses. "General Edwards regards this valley as part of his personal domain. General Maitland himself confirmed his title to it. The general is a patriotic American who intends to stand by our allies the FSE even after the, ah, departure of your armed forces."

"We can put this place to good use," Randy Donner said, looking arrogantly around.

What the hell difference does it make what we do to the lab? Dorn thought savagely. *When we pull out you'll herd all the scientific types into tarpaper shacks and use 'em for grunt labor like those poor slaves in your own valley.*

"The general will be compelled to make personal

representation to General Maitland, should any damage happen to property in this valley," Halpern said.

Dorn made a disgusted gesture. "All right, all right. I'll tell you what. We can wait till tomorrow to pull out. And we'll see what headquarters says in the meantime."

PFC Moreland and Private Lund leaned up against the closed corrugated door of the trailer box and smoked an illicit cigarette. It was just part of the booty they had received not long ago—half an hour after coming on watch at midnight—for briefly looking the other way as several figures slipped into the darkened main habitat.

"We're pullin' out tomorrow, Rick," stocky Lund said, his thick face briefly illuminated as the ember end of his cigarette flared to the inward draft of his lungs. "What do you figure the fat bastard's up to?"

Moreland grinned, his teeth pale in the darkness of his face. The sweep of his helmet cut off what starlight there was. "His brother ain't the only one who's randy."

Lund just stared back at Moreland; he was unaware the word "randy" meant anything but somebody's nickname. Moreland cursed the luck that had saddled him with this dummy for a partner tonight of all nights. There was an ounce of gold apiece awaiting them if Buddy Donner's midnight mission came off successfully, and if anyone could blow that for them it was Lund.

"He wants his little blond-haired piece. Don't you know anything?"

"Doesn't he get all the ass he wants from those worker broads in his valley? I saw one bitch brought in couple weeks ago, some kinda refugee, but not exactly starving, if you know what I mean. Her bazongas could keep you going for days—"

"People always want what they can't have, shit for brains. It's how they're put together." PFC Moreland was something of a homespun philosopher, Eric Hoffer in OD fatigues.

"But what the fuck, over?" Lund wanted to know. "We're pulling out tomorrow. Then he can take what he wants, can't he?"

"Don't you think little Suzie knows that? Just watch. She's gonna ask Dorn to take her with us, get her out of Buddy boy's reach. Dorn'd do it, too. He's a wuss at heart."

Lund sucked on his butt and looked stupid. "Get off your ass and take a turn around the place," Moreland said in irritation. "The lieutenant catches us lounging here, our ass is grass."

Grumbling, Lund pushed himself off, hitched up the sling of his M-16 higher on his shoulder, shuffled around the corner of the trailer. Moreland heard him pull his breath in sharply. There was a scuffle of feet, a quiet sound like a watermelon being cut, more scuffling. Moreland tossed away his own cigarette and unslung his own rifle, starting forward.

A steel clamp caught him by the underjaw and yanked his head back. Pain lanced through his throat, fierce and bright. He let the rifle fall and clutched at the arm that had him from behind, and then the knife blade that had been driven through his neck slashed forward, outward.

He kicked his heels and writhed like a worm on a hook. The arm that held him was as immovable as an iron bar. His chest and belly were wet. Gradually the pain faded from his throat, the panic from his guts, and then his muscles were relaxing and he slipped down into blackness.

Tom Rogers let the lifeless body down gently to the

packed earth, then wiped his leaf-bladed Gerber on the dead man's blouse. A figure stepped out from the other side of the box. He glanced up. It was Sloan, as expected, broad-bladed Kabar in hand. The front of his dark cammie coveralls was wet, and his face had a strange asymmetric set to it under its coat of mottled black and gray paint.

"Almost fucked up there, Navy boy," McKay's voice growled over the communicators as he stepped out beside Sloan. A loop of piano wire dangled almost invisibly from his paw.

"How was I to know he'd walk right into me?" Sloan demanded, indignation overcoming his nausea.

Casey came up behind Tom. In his right hand he carried a kukri, a Nepalese knife with a fat crookbacked blade that could take a man's head off with a proper swing. It had been a gift from a Gurkha close-combat instructor in the Guardians' training course, who had taken a shine to the former fighter pilot. Casey moved without his usual fluid lazy grace; he was keyed up like a greyhound. McKay kept giving him glances, but Rogers already knew he could keep himself under control.

In his left hand Casey carried an Ingram MAC-10 with a fat Sionics sound suppressor screwed onto its stub muzzle. A real bullet-sprayer with no accuracy to speak of beyond ten meters if that, his usual backup weapon. He could put a bullet through your head at a klick, but inside of fifty meters he had trouble hitting the ground. The others had H&K MP-5 machine pistols with integral silencers, more sedate but no less lethal.

"Let's get a move on," McKay said. "We got a lot of ground to cover tonight."

Rogers nodded and slipped away to check the outbuildings for Effsees. The other three ghosted around the side of the main habitat, where Spinelli and Dr.

Mahalaby had informed them most of the occupying squad slept at night.

The liberation of New Eden was under way.

The sergeant sat in the commissary down on the ground floor of the habitat and sipped hot coffee. Real coffee, confiscated from smugglers and available to people like noncoms who'd taken care to make good connections among the right people in the expeditionary force. The lights were all on, instead of just a few to save the generators. What did it matter if this place stayed within its energy ration, since it was all going to be junk tomorrow.

The sergeant looked around with regret. Not that they had to trash this place—he had no feeling about that one way or another—just that there was so little here actually worth liberating. Take the coffee, for example; here was this big, fancy place, well stocked from before the war, well tied in to the black market and scavenger circuit before the expeditionary force's arrival, and they didn't even have any decent coffee. They all drank herb tea that tasted and looked like boiled ragweed, and the occupying forces had to supply their own damned coffee if they wanted it. It wasn't fair . . .

Somebody cleared his throat behind him. He swept his boots off the natural-wood tabletop—no formica in this joint, you could bet to that—and spun into attention. The mood the lieutenant was in, he'd sack his ass for slacking on duty . . .

But it wasn't the lieutenant standing there. It was a man in battle dress camouflaged in some pattern the sergeant didn't recognize—and largely obliterated by a dark stain down the front, the nature of which he didn't even care to guess at. Its face was a devil mask of black and gray. It held a submachine gun leveled at where the sergeant's heart would be if it hadn't been currently fluttering in his throat.

Like a sleepwalker the sergeant raised his hands. "Where are the others?" the apparition rasped. "And keep it down."

The sergeant opened his mouth, uttered a cracked sound. To his fear-heightened senses it seemed a black-painted knuckle tightened on the trigger. Desperately he cleared his throat and began to speak. Very, very softly.

There were four of them asleep in bunk beds, with their weapons stacked beside the door. Holding his MAC-10 ready, Casey stopped, picked up a boot, tossed it on a snoring figure in a lower bunk. The man sat up grumbling sleepy obscenities. He piped down quickly when he discovered he was staring down the conduitlike suppressor.

"Time to wake up, everybody," Casey said quietly.

The man on the upper bunk made a quick jackknife as if going for a hidden weapon. Casey Wilson was not in the mood for the fine points tonight. The first rounds of the burst plastered the man sitting wild-eyed in the lower bed against the stuccoed adobe wall before sawing upward through the bunk and into the would-be hero on top. He gave a cry of agony and tumbled to the hardwood floor in a tangle of bedding.

Wide awake, the other two men quickly raised their hands.

With a combat trooper's sixth sense, Lieutenant Dorn came awake knowing something was wrong. He came up with his service Beretta in hand.

Unfortunately his sixth sense was a little slow tonight.

The bolt of McKay's MP-5 made a sound like three taps of a tack hammer. The .45 bullets knocked the lieutenant out of bed. McKay slipped into the room, moved quickly to his side with the weapon at the ready.

It wasn't needed. The way the lieutenant's open eyeballs glistened in the starlight spilling in the window told the story. You could always tell, somehow.

CHAPTER
FOURTEEN ——————————

Sloan and Casey rounded up the surviving troops and herded them into the commissary with the hapless sergeant without rousing the inhabitants of New Eden. It wasn't that they made no noise at all—even "silenced" weapons weren't really silent—but the lab's personnel had learned to accept random noises at night without too much curiosity. The occupying forces came and went as they pleased.

The Effsees had all been quartered on the ground floor of the semisubterranean habitat, in the southern wing where most of the staff lived several to a room. McKay made a quick check of the upper floor, then slipped down the stairs at the northern end of the building to check on Mahalaby and Spinelli, who slept in their offices there.

The stairs were dark as death, enforcement of safety regulations having sadly lapsed since the end of the world. But even before McKay had let the door slip silently to behind him he knew he wasn't alone in the well. His hearing had been whetted to a keen edge by endless nights on watch in combat zones, by half a hundred forays into the heart of enemy territory. He couldn't smell an enemy, the way Rogers claimed he could—and McKay believed him. But he could hear quiet breathing and the soft animal sounds of motion made by someone who thinks he's holding still.

McKay really was holding still. He breathed shallowly through the mouth, making no more noise than the random air currents drifting in the stairwell. Gradually his eyes accustomed themselves to the darkness. The doorway was open to the darkened lower floor, and peering through the gap between the stairs leading to the landing and down from it McKay made out the figure of a man standing on the ground floor. It wasn't a real good look, but enough for McKay to see to his surprise that the man wasn't dressed in a uniform, had on a distinctly unmilitary cowboy hat, in fact. But he was equipped with some kind of long arm.

Something funny going on. He eased himself down the stairs. The rubber soles of his boots made no noise on the rubberized treads of the stairs. He held his slung MP-5 clamped firmly to his hip, and moved so that not so much as a fold of cloth on his sleeve would brush a wall with a telltale whisper of sound.

The man was leaning back against the stairs holding a riot shotgun in a bored sort of way. Up close McKay *could* smell him, stale sweat and cigarette smoke. Had he had anything on the ball he should have smelled McKay, too, poised over him in the dead air of the stairwell. But he didn't.

With his left thumb McKay flipped the man's cowboy hat off. With the right he whipped the ready loop of wire over his head and savagely twisted the grips. The wire tightened, cutting off a surprised cry in the man's throat. McKay leaned well forward, grabbed the shotgun out of his victim's hands, then straightened, leaned back, and put his weight into the garrote.

The ranch hand's bootheels scrabbled briefly on the cement floor before McKay hoisted him bodily up in the air. He kicked for a while, and then was still. McKay leaned slowly forward again, muscles of belly and lower back cracking, and eased him into a sitting position on the floor. Then he set the shotgun down and flowed down the last few steps.

At the far end of the hall he could see another man leaning against the wall with his hands knit behind his head, his H&K assault rifle propped next to him. McKay slipped the bolt lock on, rendering his machine pistol capable of firing just a single shot until the action was cycled by hand, but making it as quiet as a firearm could be. Then he put on the fallen cowboy hat and went strolling down the hall.

The other man's peripheral vision registered a roughly familiar silhouette approaching, one which set off no alarms in his brain. "What the hell is it now, Frank?" he said, turning his head—and then the wrongness of the picture snapped into place, the curious height and bulk his partner seemed to have acquired in the last few minutes.

"Frank—?" he began.

McKay shot him through the heart. The MP-5 made no more commotion than a knuckle rapped against the stuccoed wall. McKay was next to him in one leap, caught him, eased him down. Then he unlimbered his wire sling and turned grimly toward the door of Susan Spinelli's office.

"You'll like it," Buddy Donner whispered in a voice

like a bandsaw biting wood. "Give it up. You know you will."

Pinned on her cot by the young man's bulk, her nostrils clogged with his sweat and beery breath and the cheap salvaged cologne he'd drenched himself with, Susan Spinelli writhed in a tangle of bedclothes.

She could almost believe this was a nightmare. It had rushed down on her quick and silent as a cloud of nerve gas, enveloped her as she slept—briefly, between bouts of staring at the ceiling and dreading the sunrise. Most of her fear was for the laboratory, for the lifetime of work Dr. Mahalaby would see go up in smoke, but perhaps selfishly, she was also wondering how long it would take Buddy to come for what the soldiers had kept him away from, once they departed.

Now he was here, squirming on top of her like a vast maggot, and her overriding emotion was a childish sense of disappointment and outrage: *Why did he come tonight? He wasn't supposed to come so soon. It's not fair.*

His thick tongue slavered across her mouth like a paintbrush dipped in slime. She gagged and jerked her head to the side.

"Come on, baby," he wheezed in her face, his breath like the wind from a burning brewery. "Baby, baby, baby." He sounded like a bad rock song. One hand was mauling at her groin, the other was twisting one breast through the thick flannel nightgown as if it were some kind of instrument knob. Quite a man with the ladies, old Buddy was.

Susan managed to eel a hand out from under his body and rake her nails across his face. The movies betrayed her. She'd always seen women claw at assailants' faces and leave welling red gouges. Her nails just made brief white stripes on Buddy's perpetually red face. Since she did a lot of work with her hands—there was no dichotomy between administrators and grunt workers at New Eden, and no one did more physical labor than the doctor himself—she wore her nails short. And human skin's a lot more durable than the movies make it out to be.

He didn't even notice the attack. She drove her fingers at his eyes. At the last moment she jerked her hand aside. She couldn't bring herself to put out somebody's eyes, no matter what.

Short as they were her nails dug him painfully under the eyes. He squalled and rolled to the side. The cot, which had stayed miraculously upright all this time, finally lost the battle of balance and they both went clattering onto the floor.

His weight squashed the air from her. He hoisted himself on a thick arm and turned her head halfway around with a slap from the other. During a college career interrupted by the war, Buddy'd played more than a bit of football. All his weight wasn't flab.

"Bitch," he hissed. "You been holding out on me. Now you're gonna give it up."

She lay there, stunned and sick and feeling as if her eardrum was gone, as he reared up and fumbled at his fly. *It's really happening*, pounded in her aching head over and over in time with her pulse.

His cock was stiff and he had trouble manhandling it into the open. He persevered. Then he was tugging at the hem of her nightgown. She lay on it, dead weight. He was swearing under his breath in a stumbling gabble of words, unintelligible. He grabbed at the fabric, tried to rip it bodily apart.

She tried to wiggle away. He hit her again on the side of her head. It was if a flashbulb had gone off behind her left eye. She lay there with nausea bubbling inside her, too sick to move or even to fear. The flannel tore, and she felt cool air from the open window blow across her hips. Buddy bent down. His mouth was wet.

Something flickered before his eyes. He stopped. His small pale eyes got huge. He reached up to his neck with both hands, and it took a moment for Susan's disordered brain to grasp that his weight was now hovering unsupported in the air.

Inch by inch he reared back to a sitting position. His thick throat was compressed around the middle, as if there was a seam where his head had been fastened on. His fingers clawed at his neck, and they did manage to draw blood. His little dick bobbed jauntily in the air, still rigid.

In horror Susan realized there was somebody standing behind Buddy Donner, holding him off her with a thin cord around his neck. At the last, as his face turned blue-black and swelled he beat at his cheeks with futile fists and mouthed cries for his mother. Then he convulsed and came and shit himself and died.

Billy McKay tossed his body against a wall as if he were a sack of cement ruined by seepage. "Always wanted to do that," he said, half to himself. He'd never had much use for rapists. Nor Buddy Donner, for that matter.

Susan was sitting up with her ruined nightgown gaping open. Her face was paler than starlight would account for and her mouth was working silently. Little gulping sounds came from the base of her throat.

"You okay? If you need to be sick, go ahead."

She braced herself with one hand on the floor and another on her sternum and concentrated on drawing the nighttime mountain air, cool and cleansing, deep into her lungs. After a moment she nodded.

Footsteps thudded in the corridor. McKay whipped

his H&K around, but it was Sam, looking wild-eyed with his own machine pistol at the ready. He'd half feared something like this would happen—if he hadn't been ordered to secure the Effsees first he would have made a beeline for Susan's office. Getting McKay's half of the brief conversation had tripped all his alarm circuits at once.

He gathered Susan into his arms. Dry-eyed, she clung to him.

McKay gave him a moment, then thumped him on the shoulder. "C'mon, Navy boy. We got work to do."

The sound came growling up Edwards's Valley like the grumbling of a giant bear. The sound of twelve diesel cylinders laboring under a heavy load—not too unusual a sound in mountains crossed by logging roads, but this sound was underlaid by a strange shuffling clatter, like a drawerful of the Jolly Green Giant's silverware getting shaken.

Up at the Big House at the head of the valley the officer of the watch had already gone back to his illicit crotch magazine. The sentries on watch at the bottom of the valley of the Maldita, the main valley into which the valleys of New Eden and the general's domain fed, had already radioed up that it was Effsees paying a visit to the facility. No explanation offered, not that the Effsees usually offered them, even to their loyal allies. High-handed assholes. Well, they'd be gone tomorrow. Forever, or so the rumors said.

In the big house down toward where Elk Creek flowed out to join the Maldita, Randy Donner slept peacefully with Anna Yoshimitsu at his side. The doors and windows were open; it was unseasonably warm tonight. He wasn't afraid she'd run out on him, even though sometimes—like tonight—she got a few scrapes and bruises when he used her. There was no place she could go where the hands wouldn't run her down, and the one time she'd tried he'd taught her a pretty good lesson. Besides, he knew deep down she liked it rough. A woman wanted it that way, natural-like.

In the cinder block bunkhouse discreetly detached from the Donners' two-story frame mansion slept thirty of the Donners' hired hands and heavies. The former troopies among them recognized that distinctive sound, but they ignored it and went back to sleep. They had a big day waiting for them tomorrow. Once the Effsees pulled out, they were going to make some changes in the way things were run in New Eden. Those commies had had it too soft for too long. And if that fucking stiff-neck lieutenant insisted on torching the place, they figured to do some fire fighting.

In the miserable little shacks scattered along the valley beside the fields—fields full of late-season crops, courtesy of seeds and know-how freely provided by New Eden—some of the serfs stirred at the invasion of unfamiliar noise. What it was, they had no idea. They didn't look outside, though. Curiosity was not rewarded in Manton Edwards's microcosm of what America should be like.

There was a high barbed-wire fence with a roll of razor tape strung across the top of it cutting off the foot of the valley Edwards and the Donners ruled. Originally erected to keep out refugees fleeing cities stricken by the One-Day War, it now existed mainly to keep the valley's inhabitants in. There were four stalwarts on duty in the little pressboard guard shack.

"That's something you don't see every day," one remarked as they watched an M-60A3 tank waddle up the Maldita.

The words were hardly out of his face when the tank

pivoted with the clumsy grace of one of those hippo
ballet dancers in *Fantasia*. It wiggled its butt once, as if
to get its bearings, its treads tearing up chunks of hard
earth held together by the roots of the tough, mean-
spirited grass. Then its engine roared and it started forward. Right for the gate.

Desertion in the face of the enemy, it was called. The
boys on the gate bugged for the timber. Somehow they
forgot to call the Big House and warn that all was not
well.

"Whoo-*ee!*" Idaho shouted as the M-60 trucked
through the fence as if it were so much wet toilet paper.
"Haven't had this much fun since I gave up on the
stock-car circuit."

"Don't get carried away," McKay said from the turret. He was holding on tight as the huge vehicle bucked
up the dirt road toward the Big House.

Sloan gave him a big grin across the breech of the
main gun. The confounded Navy boy was in his ele-
ment, going into battle securely encased in steel with a
big gun to shoot—well, not a big gun by naval standards, but pretty studlike. McKay was not at all so
happy about this. Like the old cartoon said, a moving
foxhole attracts the eye.

Still, he wouldn't have passed this ride up for the
world. Casey was going to sulk for weeks that he didn't
get to drive this beast the Limeys had sold them, but in
the course of his long and exceedingly checkered career
Idaho had been a heavy-equipment operator and knew
what could be known about driving tracked vehicles.
Casey had his own role in this little comedy skit.

The turret traversed left. The tank fired without slow-
ing. It had shoot-on-the-move sights and stabilizers, and
besides, as far as Sam was concerned this was like

shooting bunnies in a barrel with a sawed-off shotgun. The front of the bunkhouse went skyward in a reverse torrent of ruined masonry and human parts.

As the tank slogged on Sam put two more rounds into the bunkhouse. Men were spilling out of the wreckage, cursing and screaming. Sam mowed them down with the 7.62 coaxial. Susan's close scrape had rendered his bleeding-heart button temporarily inactive.

McKay heaved another shell into the breech and Sloan sent an HE round into the Donner house. McKay winced. Anna was in there, after all. Not that he was hung up on her of course, but she was a good piece of ass. He did hope she'd make it, but this was war.

Leaving the mansion burning, the M-60 trundled purposefully toward Edwards's own big house. "Listen to me, people of Elk Creek Valley," said Tom Rogers over the loudspeaker, giving the place its proper name. "We are the Guardians. We declare this valley liberated in the name of the United States of America and President Jeffrey MacGregor. The Effsees are running away; Edwards and the Donners are finished. You are free."

Squinting through the vision slits, McKay thought he could see a few pale faces peering out of the shacks. "Things are going to get pretty hot around here when the slaves figure out the jubilee is really here," cackled Idaho.

"Don't notice them swarming out to join the fight," McKay grunted.

"What do you expect, McKay?" Sloan said. "They're unarmed, and they've been ground pretty thoroughly into their place—"

A miniature meteor hurtled at them from the Big House, several hundred meters away. It went off in a bean field, well short, but McKay felt his asshole pucker.

"My, my," Idaho said. His standard jauntiness had been shaken a bit out of true.

"Antitank," McKay said. Fear rose up like a geyser within him. He'd seen too damned many tankers charred to mummies in his time.

"LAW, Billy," Rogers said from his seat next to Idaho, manning the radio and the bow MG. "Not much chance of defeating our bow armor."

From cruel experience, McKay knew that was true—the M-72 never had much punch. On the other hand, there was still that damned turret ring, and the hydraulic fluid—fuck it. It wasn't the locals' night to get that lucky.

"What are you waiting for, Navy boy?" he snarled at Sloan. "Return fire!"

"Aye aye, Captain."

The battle of Edwards's Valley lasted about seven minutes from the time the fence went down. Two more LAWs were fired at the tank. McKay almost lost control of his sphincter when one slammed into the turret like Godzilla's own sledgehammer, and some of the enamel even chipped off Sloan's smug pleasure in going into battle properly equipped for a change. But it didn't penetrate, and Rogers chopped the hero who'd fired it into taco filler with the bow machine gun. A moment later a figure staggered out of the blazing wreckage of the Big House waving a bed sheet on a broom handle.

McKay boosted himself out of the top hatch. A moment later Tom popped out of his own hatch like a prairie dog. Two men were just setting General Edwards down on the dirt in front of the adobe wall enclosing the courtyard. The general had been a robust man before the accident that crippled him, and even afterward he'd retained considerable power of personality. It seemed to have evaporated in a hurry. His dark eyes stared; his face was frozen like a stroke victim's. His short iron-gray hair lay matted on his skull. His pajamas smoldered in places.

"It's over, General," McKay said. The big willow tree in the courtyard was blazing, and flaming leaves dropped from it like tears. More people were emerging from the ruined house, some carrying others. "This valley is confiscated, and the folks in it ain't your slaves any longer."

The general just gave him that peculiar stare. A figure bustled up behind him. A small man, and not as dapper as usual, somehow. "This is an outrage—McKay, that is you, isn't it?"

McKay took out a cigar, picked up a burning leaf that had fallen on the turret, and lit up with it. "Yeah, Mr. Halpern, it sure is. Nice night, ain't it?"

"I always knew you were capable of desperate acts, McKay, but I never imagined you could perform an atrocity such as this! Think of the innocent people you've massacred here. Listen—" He waved an arm at the burning ranch house behind him. Somewhere, somebody screamed, horribly, monotonously. "Listen to the screams of your victims."

"I heard you liked to hear people scream, Fred. Like when they used to whip slaves who weren't working hard enough. And when the Donner boys crucified that girl you caught stealing—I hear you really creamed your jeans over that one."

Fred Halpern went pale. "Discipline," he stammered. "It's vital to maintain discipline in a survival situation—"

"No shit. That's why you and your general have now joined the ranks of the refugees. You are exiled, junior. Take the old man and hit the highway."

Halpern's cheeks wobbled as his jaws pumped. "But

the general's an invalid! He can't possibly—I mean, this is his personal property—you can't—"

"Traitors usually swing," Tom Rogers said. "Sometimes they're shot."

"Traitors!" The general had finally found his voice. He cawed the word like an enormous crow. "*Traitors.* You—you have the nerve to use that word! Assassins! You murdered President Lowell, you fought the expeditionary force that had come to help get America back on its feet, and you dare to use that word?" His lips sprayed spittle.

"Lowell sold his country to Chairman Maximov," McKay gritted. "So have you, in your own penny-ante way. Just be glad you're so small-time—"

"Hold it! Everybody just hold it!"

Contrary to the instructions shouted out of the night everybody turned his head. It was Randy Donner on his big bay horse, with his hair all wild and a crazy look on his Tab Hunter face. His feet were bare in the stirrups. He had Anna Yoshimitsu, naked as the day she was born, straddling the saddle before him, and a sawed-off double-barreled shotgun shoved up under one small, pointed breast. Her long black hair hung almost to her waist, obscuring most of her face.

"All right, you assholes, climb out of that tank or I'll blow this bitch in half."

McKay frowned. For some weird reason he remembered Anna didn't shave her armpits. Hell of a thing to think of at a time like this.

"Come off it, Randy," he said. "It ain't gonna work."

Donner dropped the reins. The stallion rolled his eyes, but the young man had trained him to respond to pressures of his knee, and he stayed under control. Donner pulled out a survival knife and dug its sawtoothed back into the underside of Anna's other breast.

"Maybe I'll saw her tit off, just so you'll know I'm serious. You used to fuck her, didn't you, McKay? Maybe I'll make a purse out of it and give it to you to remember her by."

Halpern and some of the general's other boys were starting to shift their eyes. Rogers dropped back into the tank and rolled the machine gun a little on its mount in a meaningful way. McKay smoked his cigar.

"You've seen too many fucking movies," he said in disgust.

"Get out of the tank *now*. I mean it."

"Eighty-six him," McKay said.

Donner's lower lips trembled. "Don't try anything, you shitbag. You can't get me without this slant cunt getting—"

Just about then the bullet Casey Wilson had fired from the ridge between Edwards's Valley and New Eden half a second before slammed into the left side of Randy Donner's occipital bone, plowed through both halves of his brain, and blew the right side of his face off. His body jerked. The shotgun vomited fire into the air.

The horse reared, throwing Anna Yoshimitsu to the ground. Donner went backward over the high Mexican cantle. His bare heel slipped through the stirrup. The boy was a tough customer, McKay had to give him that; even with a bullet in his brain he had enough life in him to scream for quite a while as the stampeding horse dragged him away down the valley.

False dawn was graying the sky over Maldita Peak like ash on burning charcoal. A crowd had begun to assemble around the tank and the burning house: the serfs of Edwards's Valley, silent as corpses, shuffling slowly forward. Some had things in their hands, rakes and shovels and hammers or just chunks of wood with nails in them.

Halpern looked this way and that, rolling his eyes like Donner's horse. "For God's sake, what do you people want? Go back to your homes."

"They want to see the color of your guts, Halpern," McKay said cheerfully. "You have one minute to clear out or I'll let them have their wish."

Halpern stood as if his legs were petrified. "You with the fat face," McKay said. "Monitor Lewis, isn't it? Give him a hand. Pick up the general and go while you can."

The man McKay had spoken to swallowed and stooped to pick up the general. After a moment of looking round at the slowly closing circle of faces Halpern joined him. Carrying the crippled general between them they started to walk.

The crowd watched them with hungering eyes. They looked at McKay looming in the turret of the tank. Grudgingly they opened a path.

Haltingly, Lewis and Halpern carried General Edwards through the sullen mob and off toward the end of the valley.

McKay jumped down to see to Anna Yoshimitsu.

The Big House burned to greet the new day.

CHAPTER
FIFTEEN

It seemed like a bad dream ending. The Federated States of Europe expeditionary force was pulling out. In a matter of days the last FSE troops would leave American soil.

Even though the Guardians were all too well aware their own actions had little to do, ultimately, with the FSE withdrawal, they were ready to join in the celebration. The departure was like a huge black weight lifting from their shoulders. And they had done their part. They had fought the expeditionary force tooth and nail during the whole nine months it had spent in America. The liberation of New Eden was only a last, culminating gesture.

But they found little time to celebrate. Barely thirty hours after the one-sided fight in Edwards's Valley the Guardians were sitting in the main habitat going over various plans for life after the occupation with Mahalaby and Spinelli when they were interrupted by a message their friends at Vista Systems had passed on.

The FSE occupation had been like a bad dream for the Guardians. And as so frequently happened with a nightmare, just when you thought it was over, you found yourself right back in the middle of it.

Another burning house, and one which had been in many ways more impressive than General Edwards's Big House up in the Sierra Nevada: sheets of polarized glass, big slanting redwood beams jutting out over a rocky headland that plummeted right down to the surf, and all around the forests of the Big Sur country.

Now it was just another expensive ruin in a country, a world, that was full of them. And a slight, unbelievably shabby figure sat at a redwood picnic table out on a terrace, watching without great apparent interest as Mobile One rolled up.

The two-man turret's top hatch flipped open. Slowly McKay stood. His nostrils pinched at the stink of smoldering ruin.

"Baxter," he rasped.

The figure stood up. It was wearing the mottled wreckage of a rust-colored leisure suit. It wasn't so much that the garment had suffered violence; it just seemed the victim of accelerated decay.

The man probed the substantial recesses of his own right nostril with a grubby forefinger, and examined the yield with more interest than he'd shown the arrival of a ten-ton killing machine.

"It seems like every time you come by this way you lose this Dr. Morgenstern of yours, McKay." The wind off the sea tugged hard at the words, but McKay heard them loud and clear.

Mobile One's side door opened and Sam Sloan stepped out with his Galil/203 at the ready. Baxter crowed with laughter. "You sure as hell won't need that, son. I told you, everybody's long gone. Otherwise I wouldn't be here, you can bet to that."

The Purloined Letter Method, Sam called it, after the fact. The Guardians had always envisioned Jacob Morgenstern's bolt-hole to be some sort of deep dark subterranean compound, like the late lamented Heartland writ small. Instead it was right out in the open, in front of everybody.

Even McKay could see the beauty of it—after the fact. Who the hell was gonna suspect it? A big modern house owned by one of those psychological-study outfits that danced along the rim of science, clinical psych holding hands with mysticism and cybernetics, all dressed up in a few yards of California feelgood jargon. It was a school, or a research center, or a clinic, or an ashram, or whatever. California was full of setups just like it, larger ones and smaller ones, and had been since the twenties at least.

Somehow the Institute—that seemed to be all anybody ever called it, at least according to Baxter's narrative (and slimy as he was, Baxter did know everything that happened in what used to pass for the Golden State)—had managed to keep hold of the place through the war and subsequent upheavals. The occupying power had been inclined to regard it with fish eyes at the outset, but the Institute had all but done handstands to ingratiate itself with the Effsees. It complied with all the laws and regulations the military government promulgated, duly applied for all the licenses, recoiled in horror from the very notion of the black market, even paid the taxes without demur, which damn near nobody else did.

Perhaps it benefited from the bureaucratic inertia

that had tended to keep in place the live-and-let-live
policy Ivan Vesensky had browbeaten General Maitland
into instituting even after Vesensky departed and Maitland got to be as hard-nosed as he wanted to be. Or
maybe even the post-Vesensky MilGov had twigged to
the fact that California was full of these damn fringe
groups and there was nothing you could do except step
on the openly subversive ones.

And the Institute was in no way subversive. It chal-
lenged established psychiatric doctrine, which was
maybe a suspect thing to do, but it emphasized obe-
dience to Authority with a capital *A*. The military government would never love it, but came to like it, in a
reluctant heavy-handed way.

One thrust of the Institute was to emphasize the
therapeutic function of *work*. The MilGov favored that
particular application of the Puritan Ethic—they liked
most applications of it, except when they led to actually
making money, which was a contradiction, but occupying forces don't have to be consistent. When its representatives dropped by to scope things out they were
treated to the spectacle of various worker/patients
going assiduously about their tasks.

And who was going to suspect that the snowy-haired,
lumbering man with the framer's leather apron with
pockets full of nails had until recently been a top space
scientist at the jet propulsion laboratory? That the
remarkably stout black woman troweling cement onto a
neat row of bricks was the Blueprint for Renewal's—if
not the world's—foremost expert on large-scale weapons targeting systems? That the wiry hard-baked man
with the gray-shot ginger beard and the bandanna tied
around his head whaling away at a glowing piece of
metal on an anvil was the former paratrooper, armor
commander, renegade economist, and currently the

MilGov's Public Enemy Number One, Dr. Jacob Morgenstern himself?

Nobody. Even though some of the half-dozen Blueprint personnel Morgenstern had scraped together here were fairly well known figures.

"All right," McKay said, "I get it."

Sloan was at his side shifting weight from foot to foot as if he had to take a pee. He himself felt more inclined to pick Baxter up by the front of his leisure suit and shake the rest of the story out of him. Except of course that if he put a hand on Baxter he'd have to have it steam-cleaned afterwards.

"So what the hell went wrong?"

"The Sons of Hayduke went wrong. Or one of the Sons, anyway."

McKay gave Sloan a look. "Mother fuck."

"My sentiments exactly," Sloan replied.

Being among other things a licensed medical facility, the Institute had doctors and equipment able to treat the seriously wounded, and overruling McKay's objections they had picked up the men hurt in the scrape the Red Baron's group had with Ramsay's boys, as arranged, and brought them in.

Unfortunately the Sons had a secret agenda all along. Their leaders, Mixson and the rest, had realized by the time the Guardians came back to California that the expeditionary force's days were numbered. Like numerous other groups they were willing to join hands with ideological enemies to fight the overriding menace of the Effsees. But they looked to the future too.

Morgenstern and his network were devoted to rebuilding exactly the technologically based society which was such anathema to the Sons, who felt that the technocrats and capitalists had raped the planet to the very verge of extinction. So Morgenstern had to be stopped.

And who better to stop him than the FSE expeditionary force?

The injured Son had barely been out from under the anesthetic when he dragged himself out of bed and somehow got to an unguarded transmitter. The rest, as they say, was history.

"So where the fuck do you come in?" McKay demanded. "Or let me put that another way: Why don't we just chuck your scrawny carcass over the edge of the cliff? You've admitted collaborating with the enemy."

Baxter put his head to one side on his chicken neck and regarded McKay as if the burly ex-marine had just told him about the great deal he'd just gotten on the Golden Gate Bridge. "I worry about you sometimes, boy, surely I do," he said, digging his finger into his ear. "Of course I been collaboratin'. The Effsees got hold of me and decided I was their boy for tellin' 'em what was what. What the hell'd you expect?"

Had anybody else on earth made such a confession to Billy McKay, especially within hours after the FSE had gotten its claws into one of the Blueprint for Renewal's architects and some of the Project's choicest personnel, he would have been signing his own death warrant. Baxter . . . well, the little shit was right; you *couldn't* expect anything else from him.

The animal kingdom's most tenacious survivor is the cockroach. They resist extremes of cold and heat and starvation. They endure extraordinary levels of radiation. And anybody who has stamped one into the kitchen linoleum, only to have it bounce up and scuttle away as if nothing's happened, can attest that they're virtually indestructible.

Baxter was a cockroach.

He would do anything to survive. *Anything*. He never pretended otherwise; he *advertised* the fact. And the problem was, that made him useful.

"You can't deny your cooperation led to the deaths of a number of our people," Sam said in outrage.

"Sure I can," Baxter said calmly. "I didn't know who none of them were. And, just between you and me and the wall, I never fingered nobody I figured they could catch in any kind of hurry. I wasn't fixin' to store up ill will for after the Effsees tucked their tails between their legs, just like they done now."

He uttered a ruined cackle of laughter. "Shoot, most of the time they didn't listen to me anyway. So I told them all the truth I figured was good for them, and what the hell?"

Picking a spot Baxter's fanny hadn't touched, McKay sat down on the park bench. "Jesus," he said.

By this time Tom Rogers had joined the conclave. "You were the one who called us with word this had happened, Mr. Baxter. What made you do it?"

Baxter's ever-useful finger was now stuck way back at the left side of his mouth, gouging at his back teeth. In a moment it emerged with a lump of something white stuck on the end of it. Baxter looked at it a moment in satisfaction and popped it back in his mouth.

"The Effsees are running out, ain't they? And I surehell ain't going back to Europe to mess with no Ayatollahs. 'Specially not with nobody got no more brains than Daffy Duck, like that goddam Colonel Ramsay." He shook his head, chewed a couple of strokes, and swallowed. "Thought it was time to switch sides. It wasn't any problem; Ramsay and his boys were so worked up about catching Dr. Jake they just sort of overlooked me when they pulled out. You know how I am. People just natural tend to overlook me.''

The Guardians nodded. They did know how he was. The Effsees couldn't have been too overwrought about leaving Baxter behind, unless their olfactory nerves had atrophied.

''Reckoned you boys would be a mite kindlier disposed toward me if I did you a good turn. So I started calling around for you on the radio they had here. It's in a part of the house that didn't burn. 'Course, I helped out a bit with a fire extinguisher.''

''You mean the Effsees didn't smash the radio when they left?'' Sloan asked, thunderstruck.

''Naw,'' Baxter said. ''They're a real bunch of dickheads.''

CHAPTER
SIXTEEN ————————————

With a sound like an engine starting on a cold morning the former Coast Guardsman leaned over the taffrail and spewed his morning's rations into the Pacific.

"Jesus Christ," McKay said, "whoever heard of a seasick Coastie?"

"Don't sweat it, bro'," said the big Chicano petty officer leaning against *Southern Cross*'s rail. He had on a wool cap and a peacoat buttoned up tight against a wind stiff and cold as an icicle. "Takes some people a while to get used to it, you know?"

McKay measured him with his eyes. The kid had almost ten years on him, but McKay had him a good inch of height, ten pounds of muscle, and infinite amounts of meanness. Still, there wasn't any point in getting into hassles with the good guys. At least not when trouble might pop up at any minute and spoil a good fight.

"Yeah," McKay said. "Guess maybe you're right."

McKay was never seasick. None of the Guardians was; it was one of the failings they'd been chosen so as not to have. Minor personality glitches, such as McKay's hatred of cats or Casey's general flakiness, were okay. But nothing that might render you dysfunctional under possible combat conditions, no agoraphobia or claustrophobia. Or seasickness.

He wandered forward a ways, in case Petty Officer Ramirez had any guns he wanted to clean or anything, leaned his forearms on the rail, and looked out over the restless water. *Calamity Jane*, Lori and Donna's twenty-eight-footer, was pacing the big motor sailer perhaps eighty meters away. Sam Sloan gave McKay a jaunty wave from her deck. He was glad to be getting back to his native combat environment. Maybe too glad. He had on one of those white peaked caps with the black anchor patches sewn on the front, for Chrissake. McKay reconsidered puking.

Out ahead the squat but cheerful little catboat *SeaCat* skidded back across *Southern Cross*'s bows. Somewhere, he hoped not too far astern, *Dolphin* and *Carol II*, a pair of boats midway in size between the *Jane* and the sixty-five-foot *Southern Cross*, made up the rest of the flotilla. There'd been a sixth vessel, but her engine had given up the ghost a few hours out of Monterey Bay and she hadn't been able to keep up on sail alone.

It still struck McKay funny, to be chasing an armored column in sailboats. But it actually made sense. For one thing, there was a limit to how far and fast tracked vehicles could go; they were complicated, cantankerous mechanisms that didn't wear well on the long haul. Usually a man like Piledriver Ramsay could be relied on to leave the cripples where they dropped and drive onward with the precious cargo he'd seized from the Institute—for which Chairman Maximov was offering lavish rewards, according to the youthful gnomes in Pineholm, as well as promising extravagant punishment if it wasn't delivered safe and sound. But the FSE high command back in Europe was also demanding that all available vehicles be brought back for the fight against the Muslims, and Ramsay was already in a certain amount of shit for having somehow misplaced a tank, so he had to make some accommodations for mechanical failure.

Besides, most of the southern half of California was a gigantic traffic jam, which the Effsees had made only the slightest progress in clearing up. It would take the 522nd Battalion (Mixed) a while to fight through it. And all the while the tiny fleet would be slogging south at eight to twelve knots, hoping to outpace the column and land the Guardians ahead of it. Working an ambush of the company-sized Effsee force wasn't a very promising plan, just the best one the Guardians could come up with under the circumstances.

They'd done this before, as Baxter pointed out—Baxter was stashed safely with Tom on the *Dolphin* at the moment, to lessen the likelihood of his being put in the position of switching sides again. Only that time they had run south in *Jane* alone, with only Lori and Donna for company, to say nothing of Baxter, which McKay preferred to do. That time slipping into L.A. unobserved by Geoff van Damm's gunslingers was more important than speed. This time speed was all. Last time they had tried to avoid the pirates. This time they were looking for trouble and loaded for bear.

It wasn't the way the Guardians would have chosen to play it. But the only way they'd get cooperation from the sea gypsies was to help them fight the pirates. It rankled McKay's ass to be held up like that when so much was at stake. They couldn't afford delay, and they couldn't afford to take the chance of all getting wiped out in some sideshow while Maximov got served a big chunk of the Blueprint on a gold-inlaid plate.

But as Tom pointed out it was probably working for the best anyway; the pirates had been stirred up by their newfound friends, the Effsees, and the odds of slipping past them without a fight this time out were pretty thin anyway. Best to meet them with what strength they could muster.

The strength had already been mustering in the sea gypsies' Monterey anchorage for a showdown with the pirates, which was why the Guardians had been able to promote a half dozen vessels equipped with engines. The sea gypsies, by and large, disdained "mills." The Guardians, on the other hand, couldn't afford to put themselves at the mercy of the winds, though this time of year they generally blew in from seaward and the fore-and-aft-rigged cruisers could run across the wind just fine.

Leaving Sam to play Horatio Hornblower without an audience, McKay took a turn around *Southern Cross*'s deck. It was a nifty vessel, sixty-five feet long, single-masted (*Dolphin* had two, though she was a smaller boat) with a glassed-in cockpit set rakishly back on top of the cabin, giving the vessel a real racy look even to McKay's eyes—which, while not those of a landlubber, were a lot more accustomed to the lines of tramp steamers and LSTs.

For all her size her decks were pretty crowded, mostly with the seventeen Coast Guard men crammed aboard. She was meant to carry maybe ten in some comfort, but these weren't normal circumstances. Comfort was not exactly the point.

The other boats were just about as crowded. There

had been plenty of volunteers for the trip, many of them already on hand for the fight with the pirates. Lance and Idaho had come along, and stocky Martha Gambatelli, wearing of all things a T-shirt that said "Vicious Feminist Bitch," and with a half dozen of her women warriors trailing along. McKay disapproved of women in the battle zone, but if they insisted he was willing to waive his chauvinistic chivalry and let them be some use. Numbers were going to count if they ran afoul of the pirates. When they met the Effsees—that was another issue entirely.

The Red Baron was aboard *Dolphin* with Tom. The PRB leader's arm was in a sling. Apparently the injured Son of Hayduke who'd blown Morgenstern to Ramsay had passed the word to his own buddies that the time had come to strike. The Sons in Lewis's group had turned on him about the time the Guardians were arriving at the burnt-out Institute. Paranoid by nature and philosophy, Lewis had been prepared for just such a stunt; the Sons got their asses whipped. Mixson and a couple of others got away, half a dozen were laid out cold. Lewis had lost two of his own and had taken a round through the biceps.

McKay wasn't happy about the presence of the Red guerrillas—there were lots of things he wasn't tickled about these days—but what the hell. Commies could stop pirate bullets as well as anybody. He was even less happy about the attitude of most of the expedition's members. They were dying to mix it up with the pirates. In his experience nobody looking for trouble ever had to look long.

The wind blew steadily out of the west-northwest, which meant they didn't have to use the engines much. Better yet, the weather was fair, except for occasional squalls. In the Pacific, a big storm could be a far deadlier enemy than mere pirates.

Southern Cross was crowded belowdecks, what with all the Coasties and their gear. But McKay slept well that night. He wasn't the type to brood about the state of the world, shitty as it was.

Next morning found them standing outside the Channel Islands. According to FSE traffic the Vista Systems people were monitoring from Pineholm, they had almost caught up with Ramsay and the 522nd. The day was clear and not so cold as the one before; the sky was a washed-out blue, and low-slung clouds chased each other along the western horizon.

"We mustn't get too cocky," Mario said. Mario was owner and master of *Southern Cross*. He was a retired Napa Valley grower in his fifties, with a mustache and a tremendous bald head surrounded by graying Brillo hair. His prodigious belly and skinny little legs made him look like a tennis ball stuck on a couple of pipe cleaners.

"Yeah?" McKay said, cranking up an eyebrow at him.

"We're getting near L.A. It's where the pirates nest the thickest. Like sea gulls on a garbage dump, that's how they've gotten." He squinted in toward shore, visible only as a lumpy khaki line to the east. "They'll swarm all over us. This close to base, there'll be one, two hundred of the bastards. You can believe me, boy."

"Great." Mario was one of God's own optimists. On the other hand he'd lost his only son when a pack of pirates raided into Monterey Bay in June. Maybe he had a reason to be so gloomy.

What made it worst was that he probably wasn't

being pessimistic. Just realistic. McKay shuddered and went below for some coffee.

Four hours later they came.

"It's three bells of the afternoon watch," Martha Gambatelli's voice said from the radio. "For you military types, that's thirteen-thirty, for us normal folks one-thirty P.M., and for you ex-marines—listen up, McKay —Mickey's big hand is pointing at the six . . ."

"Very fucking funny. I have to take that shit from Lori, but not from you." Though she'd done her part in the guerrilla phase of the war with the Effsees, she'd never fought alongside McKay, and so didn't qualify as a comrade-in-arms the way *Calamity Jane*'s co-owners did. "You better tell Captain Cates to haul his ass back a ways. We're off Los Angeles, and you're so far out front we can barely see you."

SeaCat was scouting ahead of the flotilla, because her small size gave her the best shot at spotting an intercepting fleet before it was spotted in turn. That was assuming they came from ahead, but you couldn't meet every contingency. The big twin diesels *Southern Cross* carried gave her twice the speed of any other boat in the fleet, and she carried the biggest punch, so she was keeping in the middle of the pack, ready to head off trouble no matter where it came from.

But it was straight ahead. "McKay," Gambatelli said, her voice unusually subdued, "I see them. Coming at us from eleven o'clock—" Naval terminology wasn't her strong suit. "Jesus God, there are a lot of them."

"Cates," McKay shouted, gripping the mike as if trying to strangle it, "get your butt back here. Now!"

It wasn't the best way to talk to the sea gypsies, who were independent-minded and cussed as mules. But

SeaCat's captain for once came back with a quick, "Will do, McKay," in his whiskey baritone.

McKay ran up on deck. He cursed—at himself, at Cates, at the world in general: *SeaCat* was to hell and gone ahead of them, three klicks or more away, just a lonely flake of white bobbing on a heavy swell rolling in from some storm way out in the Pacific. The wind had veered till it was coming almost out of the north.

In his eagerness to be a good scout Cates had bent on a lot of sail and let the wind carry him farther than maybe he realized. *Just like an indige*, McKay thought. Now Cates trimmed sail some and came about to run back to his companions.

There's an old military expression: *A good scout is a dead scout*. The rest of the convoy was just about to be treated to a demonstration of that precept.

Off to the south a line of white mounds came into view beyond *SeaCat*. Bow waves of boats coming fast. McKay brought a heavy pair of binoculars to his eyes.

"Shit," he said.

"What do you have?" Ensign Machado asked from the rail beside him. Machado was a Filipino, medium height and lean as a riding crop, immaculate in a white uniform. At his side hovered his bosun, Big Ernie, a Samoan the size of a pilot whale. Ernie had that blubbery baby-fat look a lot of Samoans have, but he didn't fool McKay; he was a head taller than the Guardian chief, and could undoubtedly tuck him under one arm and carry him like a football if he wanted to.

McKay handed over the glasses. Machado adjusted the focus, and his dark face lost a shade or two. "Ten bogies at least. Three cabin cruisers in the twenty-foot range—four maybe. I think . . . five whaleboats. And a big cabin job, forty feet at least." He whistled. "If they have anywhere near the number of men they can carry aboard . . ." He didn't need to finish.

The enemy squadron closed with breathtaking speed. The pirates had no silly prejudices against engines. They used sail on the longer hauls, but this time they were maybe a couple of hours from port, so it made good sense to burn precious fuel on a quick cheetah sprint with powerboats to overtake the slower prey. And since they would be staying out no longer than overnight at the outside, they could cram men on board without concern for comfort or sanitation, not that those were ever big priorities for the pirates. McKay had a sick feeling that the seventy men and women of their squadron would be facing well over two hundred.

Well, that was what God made firepower for.

"Ensign," Big Ernie said. "*SeaCat*'s got a problem."

McKay frowned. Once it was called to his attention he could see it too. The little catboat wasn't moving any too fast. Nowhere near fast enough to reach her comrades before the hunting pack overtook her.

In about three jumps he was in *Southern Cross*'s cockpit. "Cates! What the fuck's the matter?"

A female voice answered—Melanie Cates, *SeaCat*'s crew. A small, somewhat monkey-faced woman with an endlessly cheery outlook. "Engine's out. This just goes to show, we should have known better than to trust a mill. They always give up the ghost at the worst possible time."

McKay looked out the windscreen. Machado was blowing his little silver whistle and shouting orders, and his men were rushing inside to get ready for action. The wolfpack was horribly close upon *SeaCat* now.

"Mario!" he bellowed. "Full speed ahead! Hold on, Ms. Cates. We're coming for you."

Southern Cross surged ahead under full power of her twin diesels. She could make a good eighteen knots with the throttles open—but it was nothing compared to what the pirates could do. And nowhere near enough.

McKay wished to hell they'd had access to some fast powerboats themselves. Smugglers' specials with six meters of engine and the acceleration of an F-15 would do just fine. But laws had been passed during the drug hysteria of the eighties that put severe limits on private ownership of craft like that. Not that the damned sea gypsies with their romantic notions of the purity of sail would ever consent to keep such kidney-busters on hand.

The decks of the other three boats were crowded with people urging *SeaCat* on. "Get those people below!" McKay roared over the radio. "We don't need the pirates seeing how many we got."

"How many's that, McKay?" Lori's voice came rasping back. "A third what they got?"

McKay started to bellow and fume. They had worked this out in advance; they needed every tiny advantage they could wring, and if the pirates underestimated even their pitiful numbers their chances of survival were that much better.

"All right, all right," Lori said. "I get your point. Commodore Sam's running around telling everybody to clear for action—he orders 'beat to quarters' and I'll shuck his skinny ass overboard."

"Oh sweet Christ!" somebody screamed.

Radio discipline is just great with this bunch, flashed through McKay's mind. Shots cracked hollowly over water, and he jumped out of the pilothouse to *Southern Cross*'s now-deserted deck and squinted ahead through the spray thrown up by the plunging bow.

A cabin cruiser and a whaleboat were laying themselves alongside the struggling *SeaCat*. Jeering pirates leapt the gap between the vessels. There were more shots, and pirates dropped into the churning water, but there were forty, fifty of the bastards, and they just swarmed over the ten in *SeaCat*.

"For God's sake, use the rockets," somebody was moaning over the radio. "We've got to stop them."

McKay lunged back inside. "Belay that! We can't let them know how well we're armed!" He thanked Christ that Sloan and Bonnie Sanchez had had time to rig scramblers for the flotilla's six vessels.

"But we've got to save them," somebody else said. "They'll all die."

"Tom, Casey, Sam—anybody tries to fire heavy weapons without orders, shoot them down." He transmitted his words over his special communicator, but he held the button down on the microphone as well. He didn't want anybody missing the message.

It was a hard message. But their only chance to beat the pirates required letting them get close enough that the squadron's firepower could have full effect. If the pirates realized how strong they were, all they had to do was pick at them until they started running low on ammo, and then walk all over them.

"Holy Mary, Mother of God." It was Mario, staring over the wheel as if hypnotized.

McKay looked to *SeaCat*. A knot of pirates were manhandling Martha Gambatelli to the near rail. As McKay watched somebody grabbed her short dark hair, hauled her head back. Something flashed, and a red torrent gushed over the rail and into the sea.

Laughing, they threw the woman overboard and thrust forward Jess Cates, gave him the same treatment.

Next Melanie Cates, battling like a badger. She fought free of their grasp as she reached the rail, turned and ran aft. There was a stutter of automatic fire. She fell, skidded, slipped over the side.

The pirates cheered and hooted. And then the rest of the fleet was bearing down on the sailboats like a pack of killer whales.

CHAPTER
SEVENTEEN ——————————

The engines pulsed beneath McKay's feet, as he shouted orders to Mario. Well out ahead of her fellow vessels, *Southern Cross* veered abruptly to starboard, heeling over on a huge cushion of foam-whitened water.

McKay could even faintly hear the shout of triumph from the pirate craft. While the crews of the cabin cruiser and the whaleboat finished slaughtering *Sea-Cat*'s occupants, another cruiser and two more whalers pointed their sharp prows at the big motor sailer and poured on the power. She was clearly the richest of the prizes, and her panicked attempt to flee was carrying her in a circle well wide of her companions. The hunters lunged for the kill.

McKay was strapping a Hard Corps body armor vest on—its plates of ceramic and steel were bulkier but much better protection than the Kevlar vests the Guardians usually wore. Ensign Machado poked his head out of the crew hatch forward and gave McKay a shark's grin and a thumbs-up. The Coasties were ready for work. McKay grinned back and cinched his web belt with its Kevlar holster and several grenades over the armor. He looped the chain of a whistle around his neck and picked up his machine gun.

By this time *Southern Cross* was practically heading straight out to sea, and the hot-blooded pirates didn't seem to be wasting any time wondering why. They probably figured that soft citizens, well down on the food chain, could react almost any way when the predator panic came upon them. The big boat had changed course a few points, not yet committed to chasing *Southern Cross* but no longer making straight for the flotilla. Her deck was packed with armed men. Looking at them McKay felt his own predator's blood rise.

With a feral snarl of its engine a whaler came along-side to port. It was full of men armed with pistols, shotguns, a submachine or two, and what may or may not have been assault rifles—you couldn't tell if they could fire full-auto or not just by looking. By comparison to road gypsies, the pirates were almost sedate: no outrageous hairdos or outfits assembled of spikes and leather and hockey pads to create a bizarre effect. Just a lot of hard men in scavenged clothes, none too clean and definitely none too pretty. But that made them all the more deadly looking.

"Surrender," a man wearing a red sports headband was shouting. "Give it up! We won't hurt you."

"Pigs," Mario said, glancing sidelong from the helm.

With a thud, a grappling hook landed on the deck. Several more came looping over the rail. Strong arms began to pull the two vessels together as the whaleboat jockey throttled back. Brandishing a Mini-14 with pistol grip and folding stock, the man in the headband started to jump for *Southern Cross*'s rail.

McKay stepped onto the deck, stuck the barrel of the Maremont in the pirate's face, and pulled the trigger. The man's eyes got real wide, and then the burst sliced off the top of his head like a machete opening a coconut and the muzzle flash seared the skin from his face. He dropped flopping among his comrades as they scattered, trying desperately to escape the firestorm of bullets.

But there was no escape in the little boat. McKay had a fifty-round box hung on the M-60's side and was holding it by its fore and aft pistol grips like a gigantic tommy gun, swinging it back and forth and laughing like a demon. At hand-to-hand range the machine gun's power was awesome; given enough time and bullets you could saw down a cinderblock building with the things. The jacketed rounds were knocking parts off people, literally blasting joints and splinters of shiny bone from their bodies, and the muzzle flames set Army jackets and blue peacoats to smoldering. 7.62-mm bullets that had already passed through a couple of bodies still had ample power to smash the thin wood hull of the boat, and water was gurgling up from a dozen holes.

It was butchery as sheer and one-sided as anything McKay had ever known. Nobody fired back. Just the blast of the great black pig going off in your face was enough to stun a man. From the instant he'd blown the first pirate's head off not a man in the whaleboat had thought of doing anything in the world but escaping the smashing fury of the machine gun. A dozen men, and McKay murdered them as if they were sheep.

And he loved every second of it.

The Maremont ran dry. McKay let it hang by its sling and pulled a grenade off his belt. A pirate lunged at him swinging a baseball bat studded with nails with their heads clipped off. With the heel of his right hand McKay popped the snap of his holster flap, and in the same motion drew his .45 and fired. The man fell back into the boat with blood pumping from his shoulder.

A pirate with a blond fuzz of beginning beard on his gaunt cheeks was hauling himself up out of the bottom of the whaleboat. Both his thighs had been smashed by machine-gun bullets. His eyes opened so wide they threatened to burst the lids as McKay dropped the primed grenade in his lap.

"That's for the trick your pals played with Gambatelli and the Cateses," McKay said, as he stepped back from the rail and the grenade went off. A horrendous shriek clawed at the pallid sky, ending in protracted bubbling.

A thump brought McKay spinning around. Nosing ahead of its smaller rival, the twenty-footer had come alongside *Southern Cross* on her other beam. Pirates swarmed aboard. McKay put the whistle to his lips and blew.

Machado and his men swarmed out of the hatches. A dude in a stained satin jacket shot the ensign with a .38 snubby. The officer took a step back, grinned through the Plexiglas faceplate of his riot helmet, and blew the right side of the man's rib cage open with a shotgun.

The pirates all seemed to stumble at once. They were getting a good look at their opponents, and seemed to be having trouble believing what they were seeing.

Machado had undergone a shocking transformation from the razor-creased professional officer McKay had been speaking to just moments before. He now had on fatigues, with a bulky armor vest like McKay's strapped over them, and a fancy Franchi bullpup autoloading shotgun in his right hand. To his left forearm was strapped a Kevlar shield, an oblong curved like a Roman legionary's.

When Billy McKay was a kid his teachers tut-tutted at the bloodthirsty pirate tales he loved, and informed him piracy was dead. If so, somebody had forgotten to drive a stake through its heart. The drug wars had started bringing it back to the Caribbean and the California coast in the seventies, and many of the ever-increasing number of people made into refugees by political turmoil all over the world—particularly in areas where piracy was a rich and ancient tradition, like the South China Sea—had found it a congenial occupation. In the United States, the agency most responsible for fighting piracy had been the Coast Guard.

In the modern world the battlefield belonged to automatic weapons and computer-guided munitions—at least, that was what the brochures all said. Hand-to-hand combat was a novelty. An anachronism. It had no place in the combat environment of the 1990s . . .

Except for the Coast Guard, who routinely had to board ships and frequently had to fight to do so. And the Guard had evolved its own techniques and technology for battle in an environment where you could smell the bad guys' bad breath.

The Coasties hit the pirates like a runaway semi. Some of them carried stubby little combat shotguns like Machado's. Others had one-hand submachine guns like Uzis or Ingrams. And then there were those who relied on musclepower instead of firepower.

Before the war, the Guardsmen were only supposed to use nightsticks as hand-to-hand weapons—more effective than most people think, but not real lethal. This bunch had either bent the rules or saved up a lot of ideas that the coming of the One-Day War had left them free to put into practice.

Big Ernie swung a meter-long wrecking bar overhand

at a pirate who tried to parry with a Chinese-made SKS rifle. The bar bent the barrel, splintered the stock, and crashed down on the man's skull with a sound like someone stepping on a box of eggs. A towheaded Guardsman armed with an axe handle traded strokes with a fat pirate swinging a machete. The Chicano petty officer with the pouting Sal Mineo lips waded into the crowd with the ugliest close-combat weapon McKay had seen in his life: a steel hatchet forged all in one piece, the kind you could get in every hardware store in America, but with a few modifications, such as short spikes welded on both ends and a vicious studded knuckle-duster handguard. The petty officer now stopped the swing of a chromed *nunchaku* with the handguard, chopped the attacking martial artist in the upper arm, and then smashed the knuckle-duster into the bearded face of a pirate trying to blindside him.

McKay nodded approval. *Oughta get me one of them things*, he thought. He set down his machine gun and picked up his own personal infighter's tool, a Swiss-made entrenching shovel half a meter long, with a blade honed to shaving sharpness. It had been a popular item in the trenches in World War I, and it had always served McKay well.

With a bump the second whaleboat collided with *Southern Cross*'s stern. Mario clutched a Remington 870 riot shotgun and looked glum; the fighting wasn't doing his beloved boat any good.

Then he cried out and pointed to starboard. The big power cruiser had seen what a tough time the pirates were having on the motor sailer, and now it put its bow toward the rest of the flotilla and pulled away.

Sloan hunkered in *Calamity Jane*'s sharp bow with the sail cracking over his head. "Sure a lot of the cocksuckers," Lori remarked. She was crouching by his side with a shotgun in her hands and a slim black cigar in her mouth. Donna had the helm.

Two whaleboats and two cabin cruisers were making for the flotilla in a ragged line abreast, raising white foam mustaches as they came. Behind them the pair of craft that had run down *SeaCat* pulled away from their victim, seeking fresh prey.

"You're right," Sloan said. His throat was dry.

He glanced back. The deck to either side of the low cabin was crowded with men and women clutching firearms and makeshift close-combat weapons. Their faces showed varying proportions of fear and angry determination. Swaddled around with his own Hard Corps body armor, carrying his Galil/203 primed and ready, he felt acutely aware of the courage these people were showing, going into battle untrained, unarmored, and armed any which way with weapons they didn't have a lot of idea of how to use.

The pirate boats came on. Sloan could see the men packed into them. They were so close he could see them grinning. He felt the *Jane*'s crew tensing like a rope being wound tighter and tighter around a capstan.

"Here comes the big boy," somebody shouted. Sloan bared his teeth. They'd hoped the forty-foot cruiser would head for *Southern Cross*, fat and inviting; that was the plan, to try to get the pirates' strength stuck in with McKay and the Coast Guard brawlers. Instead it had broken off and was headed for the smaller craft.

With a splash somebody threw his weapon over the side and dived into the cockpit, screaming, "I can't take it! I can't take it!"

"Asshole," Lori gritted.

Like a man moving underwater Sloan raised his weapon to his shoulder. His grenade launcher was the bulk of their artillery. Tom and Casey, who were in charge of their munitions supply, felt that they couldn't spare many of their precious antitank rockets, not if they were going to have any hope of dealing with the Effsee convoy—as if they did anyway. *Talk about jumping from the frying pan into the fire*, he thought. *If we pull through this we'll just get shot to pieces by Ramsay and company . . .*

He fired.

A bloop of water like a bursting boil rose up ten meters to starboard of the nearest cruiser, now a mere hundred meters away. The pirates took no notice. Maybe they hadn't seen it; Sloan marveled at how meager and ineffectual the grenade blast had looked from here.

His comrades on the other two boats had also decided the bad guys were in range; two rockets hissed past *Calamity Jane* and fell in the water. One blew up, raising a slightly more impressive spout than Sam's 40-mm had.

A couple of the pirate boats faltered. An automatic weapon stuttered from one of the cabin cruisers. All at once the rest of the pirates opened up. Bullets cracked overhead, a sharper sound than the sails made, shrill with supersonic harmonics. A woman behind Lori suddenly bowled over thrashing and shrieking like a puppy hit by a car.

Sloan slid open the breech of the M-203 and jammed home another round. Whaleboats snarled by to either side. A blue-and-white cabin cruiser whipped across *Jane*'s bows. Sloan jerked up the rifle to follow it, but the rigging fouled his aim. He pulled back, got the weapon clear, but the cruiser shot by. It was directly abeam of them when a LAW rocket hit it smack in the windscreen.

The shriek of the pirate helmsman as the jet of incandescent copper took him pierced Sloan to the bone—not even a willed scream, but superheated air blasting out through the victim's throat like steam from a ruptured boiler. The out-of-control cruiser swung starboard, engine still racing.

"Good eye, Tommy!" Casey Wilson's voice came through Sloan's earphone. A whaleboat was coming for *Jane* bows on, a lean barracuda shape. Lori pumped rounds from her shotgun but the range was too great. But closing rapidly . . . Sloan aimed the Galil and fired the grenade.

The minimum distance it took a launched grenade to arm itself was ten meters. Sloan's round had gone maybe three centimeters more than that when it struck the whaler amidships. Suddenly a giant white octopus seemed to be squatting in the middle of the craft, and those it brushed with its tentacles burned, and jumped howling into the sea. But even the mighty Pacific couldn't help them; mere water couldn't extinguish the flakes of white phosphorous that clung to bodies and devoured them like alien organisms.

A figure reared up in the whaleboat's prow, back and head a mass of blue-white flames, waving hands the flesh of which melted like tapers. Lori vomited down her Washington University sweatshirt. Sam felt like it.

But just then the cabin cruiser Tom had hit, itself well alight, came crashing into *Calamity Jane*'s stern, and the survivors came swarming aboard, and Sam had to fight for his life.

The sea gypsies were peaceful people. They wanted nothing more than to pursue the quiet cruising life and leave the land to its turmoil and squalor. Most of the landlubbers who had volunteered to accompany the expedition south had similar outlooks and goals. But when they were up against it, they fought with amateur ferocity, if not skill.

The fighting had a lot more to do with the tactics of the pre-gunpowder age, battles like Sluys and Salamis, than it did with the over-the-horizon action Sloan had seen on the *Winston-Salem*. The combatants exchanged volleys of missiles, but the main tactic was to grapple and board.

During his earlier stay among the sea gypsies Sloan had done what he could to lead them along the same lines as the Coast Guard contingent. He'd taught them the rudiments of fighting with clubs, axes, and improvised boarding pikes. He'd even added a few wrinkles of his own.

The question was whether it would all be enough against the greater numbers of the pirates.

When his third rocket missed from fifty meters, Casey gave up in disgust and tossed the empty tube over *Carol II*'s rail. He was tolerant of other people's failings, but he couldn't stand to fail himself.

A whaleboat scraped along *Carol II*'s starboard flank, and Casey got a hand on the grip of his slung Ingram and pulled it to the ready position. The Sionics suppressor was screwed onto the stub barrel, not because quiet mattered, but because the weapon balanced better that way.

Idaho was at his side, his eyes obscured by wraparound mirror shades. He wore a black sweater with the sleeves rolled up to mid-forearm. His shaven head gleamed. He had a Benelli autoloading shotgun in hand.

A pirate vaulted the rail with real Olympic form. Idaho nailed him in midair. He thudded on the deck and rolled hard into the cabin, leaving a red smear on the immaculate white deck.

Idaho grinned at Casey. "It's showtime." Then the rest of the pirates were lunging aboard.

Calamity Jane's sails were burning. The things were supposed to be fireproof, but the stricken cabin cruiser still nuzzling the motor sailer's counter like a horny dolphin was burning hot enough to set them alight. Globs of flaming nylon fell like napalm rain on both sides.

One hit a woman who'd escaped Santa Monica in the wake of the bombing the year before, set her hair on fire. She beat at the flames with her fists. A pirate stuck a sharpened screwdriver in her belly, and she fell over the rail. Grinning triumph, the pirate turned to catch a burst from Sloan's Galil in the chest from two meters.

A pirate flung himself into the cockpit at Donna. She whipped up a meter-long piece of broom handle, jammed it into his sternum. There was a muffled explosion. His torso seemed to expand inside his black mesh shirt, and blood spattered the woman from hairline to belt. The man fell to the deck, moving randomly as dying neurons fired their last electrochemical charges. His chest had been blown open.

The tall woman with the brush-cut brown hair, now matted with blood, had used one of Sam's special innovations. It was a shark stick, a shotgun shell fixed to the end of a short pole with the point of a nail against its primer, set to go off when it was jammed against something. It was a one-shot weapon that required no skill to use but was devastating in effect. Ideal for somebody who'd never killed anyone before. Like Donna Lombardi. Tears rolled down her face, a little sour vomit escaped down her chin, but she took the helm again.

A pirate popped onto the foredeck and fired a burst at Sloan from a civilian CAR-15 that had been home-brewed to fire full-auto. Sloan threw himself full length on the deck, clutched at the low gunwale just in time to save himself from going over the side, and Lori hit the pirate in the belly with an axe. He doubled over it, puking blood. She kicked him and the axe overboard.

"Where is everybody?" she asked in a voice that scraped like sandpaper. She swiped the back of her hand across her sweaty forehead, smearing a streak of blood and grime.

The realization they were alone hit Sloan like a blow. The battle raged to all sides of them, but for the moment they were neglected. He didn't see any others of the ten who'd been crammed into the *Jane*. Were some of them hiding below, or were they all . . .

A dollop of burning nylon landed on his shoulder, snapping him back to reality. "Jesus Christ," he shouted, "we have to get away from that damned cruiser, it's going to—"

Right on cue the cabin cruiser's gas tank blew. Lori screamed as yellow-orange flame rolled over the cockpit.

CHAPTER
EIGHTEEN

Curly-haired Lancelot knelt on top of *Carol II*'s cabin between the pilothouse and the mast, firing a .357 Magnum revolver two-handed. A bullet hit him in the right temple, and the vessel's roll pitched him off the cabin at the feet of Casey and Idaho. He was dead before he hit.

Tears streamed from beneath Idaho's outlandish shades as he knelt to cradle his friend. "What am I gonna tell Rhoda?" he sobbed.

"Rhoda?" Casey asked, and coughed, choking on the thick smoke that hung over the sea like fog.

"She's his cousin, man."

Then the cabin cruiser from which the shot that killed Lancelot had come was bearing down on them, raking *Carol II*'s deck with automatic fire from several weapons. Casey sprayed them with an ineffectual burst from his rapid-firing Ingram, and then Idaho dragged him down the hatch into the cabin.

• • •

A cabin cruiser grappled *Dolphin*. Dodging, kicking, shooting, gouging, Tom, the Red Baron, and the other ten aboard fought the pirates for possession of the ship.

It's surprising how many places there are to duck into cover on such a tiny platform tossing out in the midst of the endless emptiness. Down a hatch—hamstring a pirate running past with a sweep of a Kabar, haul him in by the good ankle, sink your knife blade in his groin and twist. Fire two shots across the squirming body into a pirate wrestling with *Dolphin*'s stocky blond-bearded captain, four hands locked on an M-16.

Up and out—a weight comes crashing down on your shoulders from the cabin roof. Reach back, grab a handful of shirt, snap forward. A body rolls over your shoulder to slam the deck, starts up cursing. A butt-stroke in the face—your Galil has a genuine wooden stock, not something nylon by Mattel. Kick him overboard while he lies their clutching his smashed nose.

Rogers found himself leaning back against the cabin with his head pulled below the roofline. Lewis was beside him, his tan shirt with the shoulder straps torn here, charred there, spattered with blood. With a squeeze of his thumb on the release the Red Baron squirted a spent clip from his Uzi, shoved a fresh one from his belt into the grip. He stuck the empty in a pocket of his trousers.

"Bourgeois thrift?" Rogers asked mildly.

Lewis raised an eyebrow in surprise, then grinned.

Captain Wideman and five others were all huddled with the two of them on the port side of the cabin. The remnants of the cabin cruiser crew and an unknown number of pirates from the whaleboat that had helped take *SeaCat* held the starboard side of the vessel. The pirates had two submachine guns, maybe more. It looked like an impasse.

Rogers pulled a grenade from his belt. Wideman's eyes got wide.

"Stun grenade," Lewis said. "Don't worry. It'll just scratch the paint of your capitalist plaything."

"It wasn't the paint I was worried about," the captain said. "It's sinking that worries me."

"What if they got grenades?" a man with dark beard stubble growing practically to his eyes asked.

"Probably don't," Rogers said.

"He's right," the ship's owner said. "They don't want to do too much damage to their prizes."

Rogers pointed to two men and a woman. "Hold the aft end of the cabin in case they try running that way." The three went duckwalking aft. "The rest of you, get ready to go around the front. My signal."

He pulled the pin, straightened, skidded the grenade across the cabin roof, a move which required a master's touch to get it over without sending it clear over the side. Rogers had it.

Lewis was already moving. Rogers came right behind him. The grenade went off with an earsplitting bang and a sun-bright flash right in the pirates' faces. Lewis rolled around the cabin's forward end and opened up from the hip. Rogers hit the deck at his side, firing bursts past his legs.

Pirates went everywhere. Over the roof, over the rail, down bleeding on the deck. Three ran around the rear of the cabin and right up against the trio Rogers had left there. Two were cut down instantly. The third was going so fast he burst in among the defenders and managed to stab one man twice before he was knocked down and beaten to death with rifle butts and a big monkey wrench.

The deck was cleared of pirates. But before the defenders could waste more than a breath congratulating themselves somebody let out a god-awful yell and pointed. Cutting through the smoke like an icebreaker was the high white prow of the forty-foot cruiser, bearing down on them with a good eighty men aboard.

From the port quarter *Dolphin* was coming to the rescue
with her single screw churning water for all it was
worth. She in turn had just received help from a very
unlikely direction. Sam Sloan had gotten a dinghy away
from *Calamity Jane*, which was busily burning to the
waterline, and while Lori tended a badly burned Donna
he had been lying on his belly playing one-man navy
with his grenade launcher. A high-explosive round had
blown open the twenty-footer's stern before it closed
with *Dolphin*, and that batch of pirates had lost interest
in the fight in favor of trying to keep afloat.

But the big pirate cruiser got to *Carol II* first. Its engines throbbed as it backed water frantically, but its
captain had misjudged. She hit *Carol II* four meters
abaft the bow. The sailboat heeled far over amid a
crunching of wood and fiberglass.

The power boat rebounded, then came scrunching
alongside. Grappling hooks thuddded down—the cabin
cruiser was shorter than the *Carol*, but it rode higher.
Rogers and the rest scuttled back around the cabin as
bullets spattered the deck like hail. Several stayed behind, unmoving on the planking.

"Go on around," Casey Wilson was urging the slight,
dark-bearded captain of *Carol II*. "Try to get on her
tail."

But Captain Curtis shook his head. "No time. They'll
overrun her before we can come about, even under
power."

Idaho grinned. He'd lost his glasses; his eyes were
squinty and rimmed with red, as if unaccustomed to the
light. "This baby doesn't corner like that F-16 of
yours."

"Oh," Casey said. "I guess you're right, man."

Even as the big pirate craft was fastening herself to *Dolphin*'s starboard side, Curtis was laying his vessel along the sailboat's port while his crew threw grapples of their own. Casey, Idaho, and the others were sheltering behind the cabin, firing right across *Dolphin*'s decks at the pirate. Jammed in tight together on deck the pirates took heavy casualties, but they returned the fire furiously, while some dropped onto their quarry's decks, out of *Carol II*'s line of fire.

Within minutes the pirates had gotten belowdecks and were popping out of *Dolphin*'s portside hatches. Armed with a baseball bat, Captain Wideman, who wouldn't use a gun, led several defenders in discouraging them. When Wideman took a low-caliber bullet through the chest and fell back, Tom had to take the risk of setting the ship afire and tossed a grenade into the cabin. *Dolphin* didn't catch, and the blast had the effect of discouraging the attackers from trying that route for the moment.

With fire from Casey and Idaho and company sweeping the cabin roof, the pirates couldn't attack across the top. That left them to charge around fore and aft of the cabin, which meant all the defenders had to do was hunker down and wait to blast them over the gunwales when they popped into sight. The pirates were stymied.

But it couldn't last. There were just too many of them. Some of them were shouting descriptions of what they'd do to the defenders once they overran them, graphic and precise as to which few square centimeters of skin they'd peel off when. Some were shouting encouragements to each other:

"Hey, there can't be more than five or six of the fuckers back there."

"Yeah—they gotta run out of ammunition sometime!"

Crouched in position at opposite ends of the cabin, Tom and the Red Baron winced at the same time. The pirates were dead right.

"Go for it!" a pirate yelled.

A knot rushed around onto the foredeck, only to have a stun grenade go off in their faces. As they staggered around like bloating sheep and Rogers mowed them down with precise bursts of his Galil, he heard a huge many-throated shout go blasting up from the deck, and realized, in his unemotional way, that this was it.

And it was, but not quite the way he had thought. Because Billy McKay, at the head of a dozen heavily armored Coast Guardsman, had come scrambling up over the big power cruiser's stern and was piling into the pirates from behind like a huge iron wedge.

The Coasties had taken casualties; no armor is perfect. Ensign Machado had been the first to die, shot through the faceplate of his riot helmet with a high-powered rifle. But their armor and shields, their better weapons and training, had served the Guardsmen well.

Now they butchered the unarmored pirates. A stub of cigar jutting from his smoke-blackened face, McKay fired the shotgun he'd recovered from Machado dry, tossed it down, and threw himself into the midst of the pirates, laying about with his E-tool. He chopped at faces and necks and shoulders, and it seemed half the men he hit never even tried to defend themselves. They were only interested in getting the hell away from these bulky, blood-drenched figures. They must have figured they had somehow wound up on the wrong end of a Tobe Hooper film.

Some stood and fought. Big Ernie stood swaying with a finger-thick stream of blood pulsing from a bullet hole in his jugular. The battle seemed to pause as the giant wobbled back and forth for a moment, then toppled over like a falling redwood. The Chicano petty officer vaulted his body, split open the forehead of a pirate standing there flatfooted with an M-1 carbine in his hands, and the fight continued.

Like beaters on safari, the Coast Guardsmen drove the pirates forward, where the defenders aboard *Dolphin* and *Carol II* gunned them down. In three minutes it was finally all over. The pirates either dived overboard, threw away their weapons and raised their hands, or were lying around on deck bleeding profusely.

"Prisoners, sir?" the petty officer asked, helping cover the disarmed pirates with an Uzi. By unspoken consensus the Coast Guardsmen had accepted McKay as their commander after Machado went down. He was their kind of guy. "We takin' prisoners?"

A Coastie had brought McKay his M-60 out of the *Southern Cross*. He flipped open the feed tray, stuck the end of a half-belt in an Aussie ammo box inside, and snapped it shut. He worked the charging handle.

"Hell no," he said, and opened fire. It was the kind of job he wouldn't ask anybody else to do.

"You running out on us, McKay?" Lori demanded.

McKay swung a crate they'd recovered from a cache near Salinas off the deck of *Carol II*, handed it off to Sam Sloan, who stood on the deck of the big white cabin cruiser. "We got a job to do."

"Half of us are dead. We're helpless."

"We're leaving Petty Officer Ramirez and his men with you," Sloan said, after he'd handed the crate on to Idaho. "If any more pirates come they should be able to handle them."

"Maybe," Lori said. Tears spilled from her eyes. "Maybe not."

The sun hung just above the western horizon. An

eerie, heavy silence had fallen over the ocean. All around bodies bobbed on the water among drifts of wreckage and overturned boats. Now and again would come the crack of a pistol or shark stick, as somebody caught a pirate trying to haul himself aboard one of the surviving craft. It went against a lifetime of socialization for the gentle sea gypsies to act that way, but where the pirates were concerned, their mercy glands had atrophied long since.

Lori threw her arm in three quarters of a circle, encompassing the ash-strewn sea, stinking of oil and blood and burning, and the human and material flotsam that surrounded the four vessels. "Look at this!" she screamed. "This is what we tried to leave behind. Now we've brought the, the savagery of the land out onto the sea. Are you happy? *Are you happy?*" She started to say more, but instead turned and ran off for the hatch.

"Crazy dyke," McKay said, shaking his head.

Thoughtlessly Sam wiped the back of his hand across his forehead. He winced. He was burned both places, and had just succeeded in rubbing sweat through the coating of white zinc oxide ointment Rogers had smeared on. It stung like fire coral.

"Ease off, McKay," he said. "She's had a bad day." She'd lost the ship that had been her home for six years, and damned near lost her lover too, though Rogers judged Donna would pull through fine, with little or no scarring.

Calamity Jane was history, and some of the pirates had made off earlier with the captured *SeaCat*. *Carol II* was virtually unscathed, but the collision with the forty-foot cabin cruiser *Great White* had holed *Dolphin* at the waterline. A bandaged Captain Wideman was leading efforts to keep her pumped out and repair the damage. Sloan had put them on to the idea of dogging the edge of the spare sail to the gunwales and fastening it over the breach, which would require some intrepid volunteer to swim under the sailboat's keel carrying a line.

But the Guardians couldn't stick around to see how it all turned out. The captured cruiser *Great White* was faster than any boat in the flotilla—it had come through the crash with no visible damage—and her tanks were almost full. The Guardians and half a dozen volunteers, including Idaho and Comrade Lewis, were driving on.

The last crates were brought aboard the long white cruiser. The Guardians saluted and cast off the lines. The Coast Guardsmen, watching from the deck of *Southern Cross*, saluted. Some of the sea gypsies waved. Most were too busy.

With a hungry growling of its diesels it swung away south, for San Diego and their rendezvous with Pile-driver Ramsay.

CHAPTER
NINETEEN ─────────────

Under the shale-colored clouds of gray early morning, *Great White* cruised into Mission Bay. To the south they could see ships standing out from the naval station in San Diego Bay, around Point Loma, carrying elements of the Federated States expeditionary force home to Europe. If anybody aboard happened to notice the white splinter slipping around Mission Beach they didn't think anything of it. The pirates were their allies, after all, and anyway, who gave a shit what the locals got up to now?

The West Mission Bay Causeway was down, and Sam had some nervous minutes picking their way through the debris. Casey hovered at his shoulder in the cockpit, itching to grab the wheel himself, exercising every ounce of self-control he had to keep from backseat driving. McKay finally ordered him to go fidget the fuck on deck. On the water Sam Sloan was the best driver they had, never mind what Casey thought.

They passed the water gates of Sea World, where the trainers had let such captive sea mammals as they could go free. Here and there among the low sandy islands pleasure craft lay with their sun-bleached bellies upturned to the sun like so many dead whales. The mutter of *Great White*'s engines sounded oddly subdued in the stillness.

They made landfall on a stretch of weed-overgrown park a few klicks from Interstate 5. The crates from the Guardians' caches were broken open and as much of the contents as possible split up and strapped to pack frames.

"The keys are in the boat," McKay growled to Jackie Moore, an eighteen-year-old black kid and former crewman on *Carol II* who'd volunteered to come along. "We ain't back in twenty-four hours, she's yours. On the other hand, if you bug out before that time and we get left, I'll hunt you down and pull your asshole up over your head like a monk's robes."

Von Lewis laughed. "You're quite the diplomat, McKay. Did you take a Dale Carnegie course?"

"Up yours, Commie."

They set off.

The L.A. traffic jam had been preserved for the ages, ten million cars rusting on the streets and freeways of the giant city. The military government had drafted work gangs to clear up the mess, but it would have taken a dozen years to make any impression at all.

The 522nd had now fought its way right through the clogged arteries of the devastated city. It might have been possible to avoid the jam by swinging east across the mountains and bypassing the whole thing, but that would have entailed going halfway to Arizona and down through the Imperial Valley. And Maitland was on the horn hourly, demanding that Ramsay get the lead out. Expeditionary Force HQ was getting constant rockets of its own from Europe, where the situation was deteriorating with alarming speed. So to make a wide detour would be asking for trouble, which under the FSE's enlightened regime had a strong tendency to involve firing parties. Ramsay already had a large black cloud floating over his mirror-polished helmet because his single operational tank had unaccountably gone missing when the pullout order came.

Besides, he was a straight-ahead kind of guy. They didn't call him the Piledriver for nothing. For that matter, they didn't call him the Ultimate Dickhead for nothing either.

The column fought its way past Laguna Beach and began the final run, crunching along the shoulder of the last hundred miles to San Diego. Despite the loss of the M-60 Ramsay had pretty good strength: ten .50-caliber-armed M-113s, a pair of V-150s mounting 20-mm quick-firing cannon, and a Bradley M-3 Cavalry Fighting Vehicle with a very nasty 25-mm chain gun in the turret, as well as upwards of a hundred men. More than sufficient strength to guard a police van loaded with Morgenstern and the other six pussy scientists.

"A beautiful sight," he said, as he stood in his open command car watching the column roar by in orange afternoon light, having ordered his driver to pull off into a field and park. He was always conducting these unscheduled reviews; he seemed to be under the impression that his life was a movie in progress. *Dickhead*, his driver thought, as he settled himself surreptitiously in his seat and went to sleep, his last conscious thought being that he'd sell his soul for a joint.

"Ready for anything," the colonel said, shaking his head. "God, there's nothing so magnificent as war."

Ramsay's aide looked up at him in alarm. "You think there'll be trouble, sir?"

Ramsay frowned. "Trouble? No. Hell no. I was speaking, ah, metaphorically." He shook his head. "Americans have grown soft, Lieutenant. They haven't got the guts to try us. I know it's our own people I'm talking about. But I have to be honest."

"Yes sir," the lieutenant said, looking away to hide his look of relief. He was not a man in love with the notion of getting his ass shot off. And he had a very bad feeling about this whole deal.

Ramsay leaned forward and tapped the driver on the shoulder. The man managed not to jump. "Let's get a move on, boy. Time waits for no one."

"It's never going to work," Sam Sloan said.

Darkness was rolling in like fog. The air was thick and warm; autumn was slow coming to California this far south.

The sky was floodlight-bright over the former naval station to the south, and the sound of frantic mechanized activity was a constant background murmur. The naval station and environs had been nuked fairly comprehensively during the war, but the Silver Strand breakwater was still intact and the bay was still an excellent sheltered anchorage, so the Effsees were using it anyway.

Interstate 5 ran south here. Hotels lined both sides of the road, dark and derelict. To the west the land lay fairly flat, but east of the road a range of hills rose close behind the hotels, gently at first and then shooting steeply upward into bluffs densely grown with brush and trees. At the top of the cliffs stood the blocky gray buildings of the University of San Diego Medical Center.

The would-be ambushers were dug into the hills above the hotels, spread out widely to minimize the effectiveness of the overwhelmingly superior Effsee firepower. McKay was highest and central, positioned to command the biggest field of fire with his machine gun. Casey was almost as high up, off to the left. His sniper's rifle would play a pivotal role in the engagement. Sloan was to McKay's right, the direction from which Ramsay's column would be approaching; his grenade launcher had just half the range of Casey's M-40 rifle.

The indiges were strung out below the Guardians, right to left in descending order of reliability as judged by Tom Rogers. Von Lewis, the Red Baron, was first, with an RPG-7V with three reloads and a 7.62-mm FN-FAL assault rifle taken from the defeated pirates. Next was Idaho, with two Armbrusts and an XGI, the Ruger remake of the old M-1 Garand in .308; rating him lower than Lewis didn't set well with McKay, but the PRB leader had a put in a lot more time on the firing line than the versatile Idaho. Next came Tony Tiano, a leftover from Duvall's group, sporting an AKM; Rick Brereford, a sea gypsy surfer with a military M-16; a sullen young woman named Mary, the only one of Gambatelli's contingent who hadn't been on *SeaCat* and consequently the only survivor, who also had an M-16. Each of them had a one-shot LAW launcher. It was a little tough to stick the civilians with antitank launchers that would give away their positions with a flaming comet tail of backblast, but the flashless Armbrusts were the heavy artillery; best give them to the people who could handle them most efficiently. When McKay cut loose with his big chopper everybody for klicks around knew where *he* was, so it evened out.

Finally, Tom Rogers was hiding out in the parking lot of a Ramada Inn just above the road, manning the command detonators for the three big M-19 antitank mines placed on the southbound road, plus some other explosive goodies he'd spent the afternoon getting into place. It would have been preferable to have him higher, but the radio-controlled fuses for the antitank mines were specially shielded so the oncoming vehicles' radios or RF interference from their engines wouldn't touch them off prematurely, and the special sender that would explode them didn't have the best range in the world. It was one of the few cases where one of the high-tech goodies the mysterious Major Crenna had procured for Project Guardian didn't perform up to expectations.

"Why won't it work, Sam?" Tom asked.

"You have those mines out in the middle of the road, for God's sake."

They were conversing on their own scrambled cut-out circuit. The indiges had pocket communicators not dissimilar from the Guardians', provided courtesy of Vista Systems. Sam didn't feel the civilian auxiliaries would benefit from sharing this discussion.

"They're concealed, man," Casey offered. "They just look like more trash lying around."

One thing McKay had to admit, a largely deserted major metropolis was a hell of a place to hold an ambush in. You had all these neat hiding places, more than an occupying force would possibly raze or keep patrolled. And there was always plenty of anonymous trash lying around to hide unpleasant surprises in and under.

"But I always read that armored troopers were paranoid about that sort of thing," Sloan persisted.

"Ramsay wasn't armored," McKay said. "The Dickheads were an infantry division. The stupid fucker thinks he's invulnerable, and anyway these boys aren't going to be looking to get jumped this close to home."

"Maitland's getting on them to hurry it up, too," Casey added. "I don't think they're going to be real cautious, man."

Sam was a pessimistic type, and the fight with the pirates had left a sour taste in his mouth. He seemed inclined to continue the gloom and doom, but then the Red Baron's crisp voice said, "I hear something," over the general circuit.

Lying on his belly on soft cool earth with his MG to one side of him and a prepped Armbrust to the other, Billy McKay cocked his head and listened. At first all he could make out was the fidgeting of branches in the slow breeze, and the endless mutter of the withdrawing army in the south. Then the wind shifted slightly, and he heard it clearly: the unmistakable clattering rumble of armor on the roll.

During the next few moments the temperature seemed to rise ten degrees centigrade, and the air to close in until it seemed to swaddle the ambushers like a blanket. It was tension, the cheerless anticipation of a fight at bad odds, the deep-belly panic armored vehicles put into you.

It's never gonna work, McKay thought. *There are just too many of the fuckers.* They would spot the mines lying out there under their half-melted cardboard boxes. Even if they didn't, they would shoot the ambushing force to ribbons with all those enormous automatic weapons. Four hard-core heroes and a pack of amateurs, no matter how inspired, wasn't enough to beat a baker's dozen of AFVs and a short company of troops.

Headlights in the north. The clamor of treads and motors mounted with aching slowness, twisting tension within the waiting ambushers. Mary was muttering Hail Marys, and Idaho said, "Holy *shit,*" under his breath.

"Get ready," McKay commanded. He rested the

smooth fiberglas tube of the Armbrust on his shoulder. "Pick your targets, wait for my word. Keep away from the van. Anybody jumps the gun has committed suicide."

Adrenaline warped time like warm taffy. With breathtaking rapidity the column was on top of them, a V-150 in the lead, a dark police van halfway down the line of box-shaped M-113s, the second 150 and the Bradley bringing up the rear. A command car with an all-too-familiar—to McKay, anyway—figure in it jittered alongside the column. Ramsay was too impatient to ride in line with the rest, apparently. McKay hoped fervently he would be caught in the overkill of mine or AT rocket.

The column rushed past McKay's position, seeming to hurtle like a freight train on the straight. Hatches were up, vehicle commanders riding out in the open. *Too fast,* he thought, *Tom'll never—*

The V-150 in the lead rose a meter in the air on a cushion of white brilliance. For a moment it just hovered there in midair as if it had decided to become a hovercraft. Then it fell over on its right side, skidded five meters in a scream of sparks, and blew up.

The whole thing happened in an awful dead stillness. Then the sound of the mine blast hit McKay full in the face, and he shouted, "*Do it to it!*"

He pressed the trigger. The Armbrust spat its plastic counterweight out one end and a fat shaped-charge rocket out the other. A few meters from the launcher the main propellant kicked in and the rocket went buzzing off toward the rear of the column.

Rockets streaked for the column like a meteor shower rotated ninety degrees. A direct hit sent the commander of the third M-113 skyward on a spurt of flame like a cork from a well-shaken champagne bottle. Two Arm-

brusts struck the second V-105 simultaneously. The Red
Baron's RPG round slammed the front glacis of the
Bradley.

With a keening of metal treads on tortured blacktop
APCs slewed to miss the burning vehicles at the head of
the column. Two 113s collided with a bang. Spotlights
stabbed out like death rays.

One swept right across Tony Tiano's dugout. He
jumped up and bolted straight up the hill. A .50-caliber
bellowed. Chunks of earth flew up around him, and
then he shrieked and flailed his arms as the huge bullets
plowed into him.

The V-150 that had taken two hits did nothing—it
didn't fire, but it wasn't burning either. The Bradley
had veered left and stopped, but its turret traversed and
it began to chew up a HoJo's with its 25 mike-mike. The
APC commander who'd killed Tiano hosed tracers
across the hillside. The bullet stream was heading right
for McKay as he settled himself behind his bipod-
mounted Maremont, but it cut off abruptly as Casey
Wilson drilled the gunner through the helmet.

Hell was busting out all over. The Guardians were
gambling on a couple of facts of armored warfare. To
be most effective, armored vehicle commanders had to
ride in an exposed position. And armored crews tended
to panic when the antitank started taking its toll.
Nobody was eager for the traditional tanker's death,
burned to a mummy in a blazing iron box.

The Bradley had buttoned up—with its night-vision
devices it didn't suffer much. About half the M-113
chiefs had opted for safety over effectiveness and closed
the lids. The others were busting caps in their .50s for all
they were worth.

Even McKay was taken aback at how much flame and
noise four Browning .50s could make if you were on the

wrong side of them. It would be a miracle if their own indiges didn't get up and boogie; his mastery of his own sphincter was none too secure at the moment.

He drew a deep breath. *This could be it for me,* he thought, and opened up.

His burst ripped one man right out from behind his Browning. He laid off the trigger and swung the barrel for the next gunner. He couldn't risk a jam at this stage, now that the refrigerator-sized muzzle flare had let everyone know where he was.

At least two of the allies were firing their rifles full-auto at the column. They were hard-core, he had to give them that. A grenade from Sloan's launcher dug a crater in the pavement. From the corner of his eye he saw another RPG round go flaming for the Bradley.

The fourth M-113 in line was obscured by the burning wreck of the third. The fifth was driving ahead, its commander seeking Billy McKay with tracers that formed a continuous stream like a tentacle of orange fire. McKay caught his vehicle in the sights, though the .50's muzzle flash half hid it. He saw the sparkle of strikes on the APC's slab side—

The M-113 overran Tommy Rogers's second mine. With leopard reflexes he triggered it. The blast blew off the left tread, rolled the machine over completely, pinching the gunner in half.

The APC came to rest right side up, canted heavily to the left. The gate slammed down, and troopies in battle dress and coal-scuttle helmets came boiling out, dodging for the ditch on the west side of the road. The other M-113s were opening up, too, and disgorging their passengers, either through aggressiveness or the desire to get away from the blast furnaces the APCs could become in the blink of a devil's eye.

Thunder rippled along the east side of the freeway like an old-time ship-of-the-line cutting loose a broadside. Actinic white flashes spotlighted soldiers being ripped to rags by the half-dozen claymores Rogers had just touched off. The survivors dived for the ditch.

Which was where Tom Rogers wanted them. He'd sown dozens of nasty little M-25 mines that would tear off your foot—or rip your guts out, if you were unlucky enough to throw yourself on top of one. Interlarded with them were M-16A1 mines made along the classic Bouncing Betty lines. When tripped they popped up to testicle height and went off like giant shotgun rounds. The screams were audible even over the gunfire and grenade blasts.

Sam had taken out an M-113 with an active gun with an HEDP grenade. The fourth gunner had decided discretion was definitely the better part of valor and done his groundhog act. The Guardians had fire superiority —for the moment, at least. "Start moving down, Sam," McKay commanded.

The Bradley had its main antagonist's number. Its explosive rounds were hitting all around the hole the Red Baron had scraped in the dirt. As McKay swept his fire right along the disordered column, firing laddered bursts, he saw Lewis rear up on his haunches and fire from the shoulder.

Savage little explosions strobelighted the Red Baron as he did a brief spastic dance. He went down.

The Bradley's turret blew off and landed on the road with a clang like a hammer hitting an anvil.

The police van was backing and filling frantically, trying to get out from between a pair of stalled M-113s boxing it in. Casey put a shot through the driver's window and it stopped.

"Tom! Sam! *Go!*" McKay roared, as if his voice would carry above the hideous din without the need for communicators.

Tom hurled a pair of smoke grenades clear over the vacant northbound highway. Sam popped three white phosphorus rounds into the ditch to discourage any infantry that hadn't taken off when the mines started to go. Then they went bolting through the holes they'd cut in the fence that afternoon, out across the horrid openness of the highway. McKay fired over their heads as they charged the van.

Idaho and Mary were right behind them, firing from the hip. A shot took Idaho as he came over the center divider. He rolled and was up again, running as if nothing had happened.

Smoke swirled around the van. Figures rose up from the ditch as if to intercept the four. Sloan fired the multiple-projectile round he'd stuffed up the M-203's spout after his last Willy Peter and they went down. Then they were hugging the rear of the van while Tom pried at the door with a crowbar he'd carried for the purpose.

The passenger door opened and a trooper in extrabulky battledress stepped down. He had a machine shotgun with fore and aft pistol grips and a ludicrously huge drum magazine. Mary spun, bringing up her M-16. Three charges caught her in the chest. At this range there was little spread; she took every pellet.

Sam shot the man in the chest with his Galil. He grunted, took a step back, and shot Sam in the right side of the chest.

Since they were looking at close-in fighting, he and Tom were both still wearing the Hard Corps vests with their steel and ceramic inserts. Sam's saved his life, but the impact knocked the air out of him and took him out of the fight. Unfortunately, the Effsee was wearing body armor too.

The Effsee had braced himself to blast the supine Sloan, when Idaho, with blood now soaking through the blue jeans over his right thigh, lunged out from behind the van and fired. The impact of the .308 round, much greater than that of Sam's little 5.56, knocked the man back a step. The shotgun came away from his shoulder.

Idaho's leg gave way. He rolled, brought the Ruger up, and fired just as the Effsee got control of the shotgun again. The round took the soldier in the right eye and he went down blowing holes in the atmosphere as his trigger finger clenched.

The door of the van burst open, and a burst of automatic fire ripped out. Tom had dropped to his belly and lay on the pavement while the bullets cracked overhead. He tossed a stun grenade inside.

The bomb went off. Tom sat up. The van was full of scientists yelling in panic and clutching at their faces. A man in battledress was leaning against the end of the box, a CAR-15 at his feet and his hands over his eyes. Rogers aimed and fired two shots between his fingers, the classic antiterrorist double-tap, as coolly as if he were on the range.

Then Morgenstern's familiar voice of command was cracking out, ordering everyone to calm down and dismount in an orderly way, as Sam sat up rubbing his rib cage, and Tom began to help the freed captives out of the van while Billy McKay fired up everything in sight.

Piledriver Ramsay stared wildly at his adjutant. Then the lieutenant's helmet slipped off, and the colonel realized at once why the confounded young man wasn't responding to his shaking. He wasn't likely to, with that little blue-rimmed black hole in his temple. Ramsay was quick that way; a man always able to size up the situation at a glance.

With a squeal of tires the driver pulled in beside the quiescent V-150, out of the line of fire, or so he piously hoped. Ramsay grabbed the microphone and began jabbing buttons on the radio.

"Big Man, this is Dark Horse. Big Man, this is Dark Horse. Am under attack by ambush of at least battalion strength, with antitank and supporting mortar fire. Am withdrawing—will seek alternate route—"

He threw the mike down. "You get through, sir?" the driver asked, scanning the night with the eyes of a jack-lighted rabbit.

"Who gives a damn! Get us out of here, man! Can't you see we're surrounded!"

The Red Baron was still alive when McKay found him. Just barely. He looked as if somebody'd passed him through a garbage disposal.

"We won," he said. The classically chiseled face was still intact beneath its coating of blood and grime, but it was the only part of him that was.

"Yeah. We won." McKay cradled his head and poured water from his canteen between his lips. You weren't supposed to do that with internal injuries, but Lewis's guts had been strewn over enough of the bushes that he figured they couldn't rightly be called internal anymore.

"You got the scientists?" Lewis was looking off at nowhere in particular, but his voice was firm.

"Yeah. Sniper got one, but Tom's loading the others into the truck we got running, up at that shopping mall half a klick down."

"So. You capitalist lackeys"—a wince followed by

a grin—"you win again. Well, better you than the damned fascist Effsees. And these scientists will undoubtedly do work to benefit the . . . proletariat, in between dreaming up new weapons of mass destruction, I'm . . . sure."

There was a blast from across the road. McKay ducked briefly. *Somebody's found another of Tommy's mines.*

Fingers grabbed his collar, surprisingly strong. "I . . . told you. I told you I'd help you till—till this was over."

McKay nodded. "Yeah. And you were right. You did the job for us, Baron." He found he didn't begrudge the man the words.

"You won now. But we'll win"—a spasm of pain lifted his shattered torso off the ground—"in the end—"

He fell back. Slowly his fingers released their grip on McKay's coveralls.

"The hell you will, Commie," McKay said, and stood.

"We're ready to go, Billy," Rogers's voice said in his ear.

McKay looked off to the south, where the Effsees were pulling out. One menace was over, but he knew there were many more battles to fight before America would be free again.

"I'm on my way," he replied into his communicator.